FISSION

KSHITIJ DUBEY

WOW Book Publishing™

PROLOGUE

A man in a grey suit with greying hair and what seemed like a grey personality entered the room. There were no windows, and a single bare bulb lit the room. A single door; seven inches thick, and could be locked remotely. It was almost as if it was a prison cell. The man was carrying a briefcase. As he sat down at the table, he propped it against the table leg. He waited for the next person to arrive, looking calm and almost bored.

When he did, he tried to be quiet, but the sound of his leather-encased feet slapping against the floor filled the room. He sat down loudly on the other chair, and pulled it in, propping his elbows on the table.

"So, you have the items I requested?" the new arrival requested.

"Of course."

"Let me see now."

His English was acceptable, but was clearly his second language."

"Of course."

The grey man snapped the briefcase open after entering the code, and turned it round. Inside, a single pistol, four magazines of bullets and below them five hundred thousand dollars in cash. The man held one to the light to examine it. Satisfied, he replaced it, then took the briefcase with him.

"And the other arrangements?"

"You will have the troops at your base within a week, and the final item you requested will be ready within two weeks."

"Two weeks? What are they doing in that little factory? Baking cakes?"

The man shrugged, and responded as impassive as ever.

"They're working on my command. You will receive the item within two weeks."

The other man grunted. He was actually very pleased right now, but it wouldn't do to show that now. He smiled to himself. It was a dream come true for him today.

CHAPTER 1

The sun shone upon the wasteland that used to be Washington DC. All of the buildings gone, the towering skyscrapers reduced to broken and jagged edges. Rocks were piled up everywhere, towering boulders were ground to mere dust, and the wildlife was nonexistent. Dust and sand swirled around, forming neat circles onto the once lush ground, and all the landscape was bleak; hills and grass all replaced with a dull brown. The winds were of hurricane strength; whistling past, bending whatever trees were left. Huge sandstorms floated across the barren ground, and the buildings were relentlessly beaten by the wind and sand, the glass shattered, the outside weather-beaten and raw. It was as if there had been an earthquake, hurricane and tsunami, then the sun melted it down, all at the same time.

Adam woke laying spread eagled on his stomach, and his ribs, calf and thigh muscles were cramped, and the circulation to one of his fingers had been cut off. There were also raw patches of skin on his back and legs, and every time his damp shirt made contact with them, jolts of pain went coursing throughout his broken body. Groaning, he pushed himself onto an elbow, and experimentally flexed his fingers and toes. *Nothing missing,* he thought. He got to his feet, and looked up at the broken city. His tired mind couldn't comprehend the scale of the disaster in front of him. Dust stung his sunken eyes, and he closed them again. He fought against sleep, but he was still *so* tired.

So tired.

Sleepy.

Adam collapsed, and he was gone again.

When he woke up, he'd half-expected the situation to be a dream, but those expectations were dashed against the barren ground. Adam forced himself to get up again, but his tired limbs were as heavy as lead. *I need to get up now.* There were small, miniscule pebbles being flung past him by the wind, but there were more than just pebbles. A boulder was being thrown down the broken streets, and it was hurtling towards him at a frightening speed. Adam forced one more, final effort out of his legs, and threw his body awkwardly out of the way., The boulder caught the sole of his shoe, ripping it off from his foot. His body was exhausted from the single effort, and he fell into a fitful sleep again, hoping against hope that he wouldn't be as tired when he woke up again. He twitched in his sleep, and rolled over on the rough, unforgiving ground.

Adam was sixteen, and although most people that his age have no sleep schedule, Adam he did. He had a sleep schedule at least. Before, whatever killed off everyone else in the city, reached him.

When he woke up, he felt more refreshed. He couldn't see anyone, and despite his hunch that everyone was killed, he still called out.

"Hello? Anyone there? HELLO?"

Adam knew that there was nobody else around him for miles, and he gave up the calling out. He pulled himself to his feet, and began to explore the ruined city.

The entire state was reduced to rubble, pieces of concrete on asphalt and broken pieces of glass on the floor, making sure that Adam stepped carefully. He walked through the ruins, marvelling at the extent of the damage. A few of the remnants of the buildings were still identifiable. A crosspiece from a ceiling. Ceiling tiles. A photo frame. Adam leant forward and picked it up, and he saw a whole family, happy as ever. His thoughts turned to his own family. He realised that they weren't here, that they were dead from whatever happened. It was the only logical conclusion that could come from this situation. He was truly gutted about the fact, but Adam knew that if he spent his time crying now, he wouldn't be able to find shelter at all, and he would find himself outside, with no protection from the sweltering heat, and no water or food. And it seemed as though that was the case. He already longed for some water, his throat itching and burning, and his eyes watering. Adam continued walking through the ruins, until he reached what could have been a park, the hinge of a metal fence laying on the ground with nothing to support it, the screws still encased in what might have been mortar. He saw what could have been a large patch of grass, but none of that existed here. All of the green was gone, the bushes dead and the swing sets rusting away, the slides knocked over and some missing. It was a stark reminder of this situation, and Adam wanted to leave as soon as possible. It saddened him to see a place that once was full of energy disposed of that way. He shook his head clear of the dark thoughts, and walked out of the park, and continued on his way. He didn't know why he was still walking, but a small part of him thought that there might be someone out there, willing to help him out. But as he walked, he just felt more sadsadder and sadder. The capital city! Reduced to this. It was incomprehensible to him.

Adam could imagine the landscape looking dystopian and movie-like from above, but when inside the city itself and not above, it was harrowing. Adam was also aware that he would probably die from dehydration very, very soon. *Great, dying in a dystopian city with no friends because I don't have what makes up seventy percent of the planet. Just how I wanted to go out,* he thought. After collapsing once, he found an unopened bottle of water laying on the ground outside of a ruined store, except but it was leaking on leaked on the store shelf, and there was barely a trickle of water left. Adam sighed at his bad luck, but drank it anyway. Unfortunately, the water served only to remind him that he was thirsty. He moved onwards along to see if he could find anything even more useful, like slightly more than a single millilitre of water. As he trudged on, he looked around at monuments, and he felt like he was on a tour of Washington, except without the tour guide, or the tourists, or the cars, or the shops, or anything, just the shattered remains of a city.

I remember this place... He was standing on a path, going around what looked like a city square. In the centre, there was a small island, and on it was a massive elevated cube with a large staircase going up. The staircase went nowhere, oddly, and there were tiny fragments of glass and marble on the floor., but only small, small pieces. This odd structure was overlooking another building made in a similar fashion, but shorter and wider, with what looked like pillars coming out of the ground. It was about a mile away. With a jolt he realised where he was. "The Washington Monument," he muttered aloud, which would mean that the other building was the White House. *How has this happened? Where are all of the buildings? The grass, the shops. Where is everyone?* They were the only questions on his mind, but he couldn't find a solution to it all.

He continued walking walked onwards, the dust billowing around him, and the sun's glare shining in his eyes. While he walked, he was acutely aware of his state of still aware of the countdown until dehydration, the clock ticking in his mind's eye, following him, and Adam felt the first grips of fear close in on his heart. Every step seemed as if it was getting harder and harder to take, and his breathing became more and more ragged. His legs buckled occasionally, and he felt slightly faint. All signs of dehydration, he knew. He was also feeling also felt the first pangs of hunger, and Adam knew that extreme hunger could leave someone lying down, unable to move from the cramped muscles in his stomach. Adam grew more and more frightened, as though a single touch could kill him, and theoretically, it could. He forced himself to not hyperventilate, as that would use up the little energy he had, and he forced himself to keep calm, as he tried in vain to find more water.

Since he knew where he was, the White House, he knew that to get water, his best chance would be near where he was, since lots of people would make money selling essentials near monuments like this. But the result was grim. The ice-cream stands were ruined, the freezer fluid leaking, and the ice-cream more like sweetened-sugar-flavoured-milk, and the water bottles had burst. He even looked in a store cupboard of one of the shops, but all of the water bottles had burst and dried up. *Very strange. Possibly a shockwave?* It seemed likely, and suddenly Adam knew. He could remember what happened; he must have had a temporary concussion. He saw something flying out of the sky, the screams, and he began to run in the opposite direction. The blast would be a few kilometres away, but the people didn't know that and they ran towards it, in confusion and eagerness to get the first photographs onto social media. But Adam and very few others knew that it wouldn't be good, and they ran, fast and hard harder and harder, but they weren't used to such running and soon were forced to stop, falling on the pavement, and getting stampeded by the other people. Adam went harder, and even faster harder, and he remembered feeling the awful vibration as the area of impact was vaporised. He had been a few kilometres away, and he kept on going, trying to outrun the inevitable shockwave. He didn't, but while everyone Dwas flattened, and some of the buildings collapsed, he was hit at a weaker point in the shockwave, and he was flung into the air like a rag doll, and fell hard on the ground, lying on his stomach where fuel landed on his back, searing his skin. He turned over, and lay there, staring up at the hideous mushroom cloud. Then out of nowhere something hit him below the ear, and he was knocked out cold, which was how he had gotten the concussion. It had been a nuclear bomb. It all made sense now, and he knew that almost all of the water in the city would be poisonous, but radiation poisoning took a while to settle in, and drinking anything would be more important than worrying about it. Even though he now knew what had happened, it wouldn't help if he was killed by dehydration in twenty minutes flat. He smiled inwardly at that, but it was more out of irony than actual humour. He looked up, and almost dropped to the ground in shock. He'd found a shop, which was ruined, but there were sealed items inside, and Adam could make out the remains of a sign that said, "SURVI". It looked as if it was a survival gear shop, where you would find coats, shoes and more, but all Adam could find was a water purification system. You poured water into the funnel, and it cleaned it until it was fine to drink. He'd taken it; nobody was going to arrest him now. He just had to find some water. He was looking for puddles, or taps or sinks in buildings. He only had time to check two or three buildings until he would collapse from lack of water, and soon die.

The first building he checked looked like it had been an office building; it was tall and there were lots of empty panels, which showed lots of glass. He saw a security post, where you had to present a card and the machine would let you through, but in this case all he had to do was vault over the waist-height exit door and he was inside. He found the bathroom easily enough, and he held out the funnel under the tap, then, crossing his fingers, he turned the tap on.

A steady stream of water came out, brown and muddy, and drinking directly from there wouldn't have been a very tasteful way to die, but with the filters, it came out considerably cleaner than before. It all went into a cup provided in the kit, but there wasn't a lot of water in there; enough for him at the moment though. The pipes were soon empty, and the water stopped flooding out, and once every drop had been oozed out of the system, he drank the lot in a single gulp, and the wonderful feeling of lukewarm, metallic water going down his paper-dry throat blessed him. He intentionally left some of the liquid, and poured it onto his face, reviving him a little. He now had some time on his hands, and the fear that had been holding on so tightly left Adam now, and he felt free. But only for a second though, as the dusty air was plastered to his throat, and now it was only marginally wetter than before. As he walked, he spotted the remains of a supermarket outside of what would be the blast radius, and the stuff in the very back was clean. Adam ate sparingly, and took food and some essentials with him.

He was fed, and no longer thirsty now, and even though there would be radiation in the packets and the water, it couldn't be worse than laying unconscious for several hours in an irradiated city, then spending even more time in the city. Now that two out of three of the goals were secured, he needed the final one; shelter. He could hide out in the buildings, but that would be cold, dangerous and depressing. There was barely anything he could do, and he could feel himself weakening, not from lack of food or water, but from the radiation. Adam knew that after about a day, with constant exposure, it would become serious, and there wasn't much Adam could do about that. He had to get out of the radiation quickly, but if the radiation was still strong this far from the original impact point, then Adam would have no chance at all. He realised that either way, things didn't look very good for him.. He still conserved food, but he decided that he would at least want to see how the impact zone looked like; after all, it's not every Tuesday you get to see and experience an actual nuclear blast. There could be people there, after all.

He took his stuff, now all in a large rucksack on his back, including all of the foodstuffs he'd acquired, even though they would be poisonous, and set off. Adam knew generally where he was going; there had been a great big mushroom cloud in the air, and there was still some trace of it now. He'd also found some tattered trainers, but even though there were holes, the sole was intact, if a little bit worn. Now he didn't have to worry about glass. He made ground quickly, and the stages were clear. As he went closer, the buildings became weaker, the dust more evident, the lack of life emphasised by the corpses on the streets and in some of the dead of both humans and wildlife. Adam turned a corner and stared in shock.

There was … nothing. It was just dust and sand, blown in from somewhere else. There were dust-storms on the horizon. Small patches of rubble were seen. He realised that he'd been on the outskirts of the city; the fireball had vaporised everything in a radius of quite a few kilometres. There was nothing there at all, and Adam could almost feel the radiation going down his throat. It had been bad on the outskirts, but here, it was definitely lethal, and he could die much quicker here. He was about to turn and go back, when he saw something on the horizon. A small shimmer. He would have left it to heat, or some weird gases, but he was interested by it now. He trudged through the sand, but after four steps he realised that he would be encased after another ten. He came back out, and marked this spot with a tear of material from the tarpaulin on a stick. It should signal him. He turned around, and ran to the nearest intact shop, which was a small while away; about two kilometres away.

He'd taken a snowboard. He fitted the straps, and pushed off. He got a few other supplies too. He'd applied a low-friction gel, which he had found from the same store he'd scavenged the board from. He put it on the bottom and let it harden, so that the sand would just slide off of it. He pushed off, and made his way towards the haze, but then saw it disappear. He was intrigued now, and he continued on his way.

Once he reached his marked place, he saw nothing. Just the bleak landscape, nothing more. He realised that he'd wasted his time here, and it was probably just a heat haze. But he didn't want to leave it. He took a small rock from the sack he carried, and lobbed it as far as he could. It hit something, and bounced off. Except it had hit thin air and ricocheted off at an angle to his right. *I saw this sort of thing on television; they have cameras, and they send the feed to the screens, making it look like there's nothing; its just empty. But there's got to be something inside.* He held a small amount of water in his pack, and he knew that this would be a waste, but if this worked, then he knew that it would be either safe or unsafe to try and get into the structure. He spilt some water on where he thought there would be a screen, and waited.

He'd been lucky, since he poured it right where two screens happened to join, the water slipped in and one of the screens started spitting sparks. It was rectangular, and it suddenly switched off, and it was a clear black screen. Some of the others had sustained water damage, and they were fizzling in and out of focus. He kicked through them, and came face to face with the muzzle of a gun. It fired. Adam thought he could feel the pain ripping through him, but it was a dart that penetrated his skin, and he looked up to a group of around seven or eight people, standing above him, in all black, some of them wearing visored helmets, some wearing gas masks. He croaked feebly, but they just picked him up, and began walking somewhere. After that, his mind gave up the struggle.

CHAPTER 2

A clock ticking evenly and quietly woke Adam up. He sat up, to find that he was in a blank, whitewashed room, with a toilet behind a screen and a small wooden desk to one side, a rickety chair tucked underneath. *"Where am I?"* he wondered. In one corner, he could see a small camera, a red light winking at him. "Hello? Anyone here?" he shouted. Nobody came in through the door. Adam went to the door and tried it. It was locked. Seeing he had nothing to do, he sat down on the padded floor and waited.

He was frustrated after an hour. He was hungry again, so it had been over a day, and he was also parched, his head spinning from the lack of water. His body ached, and he realised that he'd walked more than a marathon just the previous day, and that he had over-exerted his body so much that it wouldn't function properly. Just to add to his mood, he was coated in the dust and grime from the wasteland. There was only one thing that pushed against his mood, and that was that he didn't feel any effects from the radiation. *They must have given me something to counteract it,* he realised. The fact still remained; he had been shot at, abducted and healed, all against his will, and was being held a 'comfortable' prisoner in this room. Adam felt like smacking his head against a brick wall. He couldn't even do that here with the padding on the walls. *I'm not a psycho,* he thought to himself. But then he realised that he wanted to smack his head against a brick wall. *I think that qualifies as crazy.* But still, he waited as patiently as he could, the small camera in the corner still watching him like a hawk.

After what seemed like three hours, the door finally opened. There was a small robot, on spotlessly clean tracks, and it crawled over to him. It had a tray in its hands—*claws? Robot things?*—and it was piled with clean, cooked, warm food; pork chops, boiled vegetables, and *fries.* Actual fries in an apocalypse. once he'd finished, he licked his fingers and tentatively put the tray back in the little robot's arms. A small button extended from what might have been it's head, so that Adam could see it. It said 'PLAY'. Adam pressed it. A voice came out, and Adam could tell that it was a live feed, and not a pre-recorded thing. He spoke, but his voice was a croak, as he realised that he hadn't spoken in a while, and the dust had dried on his tongue. He drank some more water that had been on the tray, then tried again. "Hello?"

"Welcome Adam, to the headquarters of... well, we haven't gotten round to picking a name yet. This building here is called the Arrowhead."

Adam was so shocked that they knew his name, he didn't listen properly to whatever else the man had to say.

"How do you-"

"Questions at the end. We have many purposes, like going out and rescuing people from the outskirts of Washington DC, where they weren't vaporised by the blast that I'm sure you're aware of. We also apologise for the rough treatment you suffered from the hand of our men; they thought you were a spy."

"Spy? For who?"

"There is a group just outside of Washington DC; they are antagonising survivors, and raiding stores in the city. The north-western area of the city is completely cleaned out by them, and they were moving on the south side of the city when you turned up. You could say that the group are terrorists, and we are fairly sure that they launched the bomb on us; after all, they are the only other people in the wasteland. We have evidence that it was quite powerful, maybe 40 megatons."

Adam had no idea what that meant, but before he could question it, he was interrupted by the voice. "This building survived the blast, and that is all that we know of the situation.

Adam wanted to ask how that was possible, but he stopped himself. There were many possibilities, it could have been buried in one of the hills that were now dust and sand, and propelled upwards by a platform, or they could just be fast builders. Whatever the case, Adam was fine without the knowledge.

"As I'm sure you understand, you have been rescued from the wastel-"

"Actually, I was taken in rather unwillingly."

The voice coughed, then moved on.

"Wasteland, so you are quite… grimy. The shower block is out the door and to the left; it's clearly labeled, the door is unlocked now. You can wash in there. Oh- you need your access card. Here it is." The robot ejected a small card like a console would eject a disc.

The voice suddenly cut off, and the robot-machine-thing wheeled itself out of the door—Adam could have sworn he saw it wink—and left the room. Adam stayed, processing what he had heard and aligning it to what he had found out. It made perfect sense; the whole lot. He pushed it out of his mind, and looked forward to his first shower in a week. He threw the door open, and walked outside and to the left, and he saw the door. He went in, and immediately noticed that the room was miniscule. There were only four or five showers in there. *Enough for an army? I've seen barely more than 6 people in this building; surely not enough space here for even that much.* He didn't remember seeing any other buildings apart from the massive concrete block, which he'd only seen briefly as he blacked out. Putting all of this out of his mind, he chose a cubicle, and set to work making himself human again.

Once he finished, there were clean clothes provided on a bench. He pulled them on, first a pair of jeans, then a T-shirt that was a plain black; no designs, and no labels. He found some soft, white socks and a pair of running shoes. Somehow, all of it was the right size, as though it had been tailored for him. Strange. He did up his laces, and walked out of the shower block. And that was when he began to question his own sanity. In front of his eyes, he had seen the little table outside of the room, but it had been empty. Now, there was a small device and a pair of headphones, and a small note that said, "Put them on"

He complied, and a voice wafted out of the speakers.

"Welcome to the tour. You must be outside of the shower block used only by the new people, since you don't have a room as of now, so face the door and turn right. We will begin the tour now." The voice was robotic, and yet it definitely sounded humanoid. Strange. It was a little bit eerie, and for once he felt just a little bit alone in this place. He hadn't actually seen anyone; just masked figures in black. No faces.

"Follow the corridor, and you'll see the first door to your left is the door to the emergency staircases. As you must know, these are used in case of a fire. There are doors in the same place on all of the other floors. They are locked unless there is a fire detected, or the emergency alarm goes off. Moving ahead, you can see the elevators. Scan your ID card on the scanner and an open elevator will present itself." Adam noted the small, almost invisible grey scanner built into the wall.

"The elevators have infrared sensors, so if more than one person enters the elevator without scanning, then the doors split open to the full width, and the rear wall pushes them out of the elevator, and as soon as they are seen to be out, the doors close." Funny, he thought.

"Since you have an ID card on you, scan the scanner and go up to the 4th floor. The basement is for the prison cells, although they aren't used, the ground floor is used for the proactive sector; things like the armoury, shooting range and hospital wing. Second floor is used for the gym mainly, with the cafeteria taking up a good amount too. Third floor, which is where you are right now, is used for accommodation and such, while the fourth floor is for the higher-ups, and also is home to the massive laundry room. You aren't actually allowed up there though; the people who work there take a private way up." He'd pressed the button as soon as the man had said that, and he cursed him in frustration, while also seeing the funny side to it. The man was saying, "The elevators go up there, and they are repelled by magnets at the top. When they can't make it to the top, they give up and go to the basement floor." Adam couldn't help but chuckle as they stopped rising, but the smile was wiped off of his face as they plummeted straight to the bottom. He seriously thought that the elevator had gone into free-fall, but then the voice said, "The elevator also temporarily detaches itself from the rails. Just to add that… punch." Adam felt the elevator grind to a halt as the elevator clutched back onto the rails and they slowed down. Adam got out of the elevator at the basement floor, and waited for the voice to do something. It started rambling on again. Adam really was hating this tour now.

After hours and hours of being sidetracked and lead to dead-ends made for the sheer purpose of the tour, he finally reached the end of the tour, exactly where he had started. Just before he tore the damned headphones off, he heard the voice say one more thing. "Well done, you made it without quitting. Very strong." Adam sighed inaudibly, then tossed the device into a nearby bin built into the wall. It hit the back with a *CLANG* and dropped somewhere in the depths of the garbage system. He got up and began to walk to his room, when he realised that he didn't know where it was. For all of this touring, he had nowhere to go afterwards. He snorted, more in derision than humour, and then decided "A walk never killed anyone. Right?"

* * *

The man who had hired him as a waiter and butler was strange, he thought. Different. The butler was barely thirty years of age, and was quick on his feet, but this man scared him. Not a lot of things scared him; he was overconfident and pompous, but all of that bravado had faded when he had first seen his employer. With a distinctly broken nose that he hadn't bothered putting back in place, and a beard that looked unkempt but was neatly trimmed, he looked like a stereotypical street fighter, somewhere far east. But he wasn't new here. He had scars all over his face, his hair barely masking any. A knife wound here. A faded bruise there. A slightly bent jawline. It told the butler that he was far, far outmatched, since someone who lost all of his battles would look dejected, but this man looked far, far from it. From what he had gathered from him, he had a very short temper, and was obviously very strong and experienced, just from looking at his weather-beaten face. He'd tried to act polite, but he found his arms shaking when he was with him, and soon found that he paled visibly when he even thought of the wretched man. He knew that he shouldn't be intimidated; he was a military commander after all, and yet he was able to crawl under your skin and stir fright from within. He felt trapped, like a caged tiger, in the clutches of a giant. He wondered now why he had even considered accepting the offer; the money had been to pull him in. But there was no place at all to spend it, not here. And he was forbidden from leaving. *What a waste of my life* he thought to himself daily, but the mute terror in his eyes was definitely apparent to his master. He heard a name once, through a door. The word haunted him for the rest of his life.

Khan.

*   *   *

Adam gave up on walking. He hadn't found anybody else apart from a few, unsmiling adults, and he realised that it must be night. He hadn't actually checked his watch. Sure enough, the time was about 11 PM. Sighing at his own stupidity, he walked back to his starting point to find a new note on the bench at the shower block. This one read, "Room 207".

Adam tossed this into the bin as well, before making his way to the room. The corridors were long, and it almost felt like a maze if you didn't know where it was or had the oh-so-helpful tour.

At least the accommodation is nice, he thought, as he scanned his card and entered. It was clean and spacious, with floor-to-ceiling wardrobes and windows. Adam half expected the bed to be floor to ceiling too, but it was a simple double bed with a spring mattress. An inconspicuous door led to the en-suite bathroom, with clean tiling and a shower. He showered again; he could still feel the dust on his skin, and sat down on the bed. He realised that this was the first time he was sleeping safely for about a week. He put it all aside and forced himself to sleep, even though he didn't feel tired at all, to try and gain some energy for tomorrow.

CHAPTER 3

Adam was beginning to slot himself into the daily routine of things, and he instantly observed that people here didn't talk much. Most of the people were very self-centered, and he didn't hear any of the conversations that usually would happen around a "normal place". He understood that there had been a nuclear blast, and most of the people in their families were dead, but the lack of noise was unsettling, to say the least. It seemed as though people had no interest in talking at all, like they had been silenced by the blast. Adam wondered if they thought the same things, or if they were just hollowed out, empty from the blast.

The cafeteria was beautiful, just like he'd seen it briefly in the tour. With soft, fabric chairs instead of the plastic ones you get in school, which seem to be moulded for maximum discomfort, and hardwood tables which would have been made from the ruined trees. Lots of people milled around the cafeteria in the morning, but occasionally if Adam was early, he would spot a few people in black uniforms, similar to the people he'd seen when he was swarmed by the mutant creatures. He knew that they would have been somewhere here; after all, they saved him, but he didn't expect them to be a part of the running of this place so deeply. He realised that he didn't even know who 'they' were after all. Adam also spent time in the gym, unlike the others in the building. He also used the swimming pool, which was heated or cooled depending on the temperature. A waste of time if the entire building is air conditioned and nobody goes outside. Nevertheless, he usually swam every day, doing laps over and over again. It felt good to him, as though he was washing the grime of living, off from himself. There were other places to pass the time away as well, and it felt like a large mansion. The most intriguing parts of the building were the ones that fully displayed the advanced technology that he'd seen when he first came here. Every piece of clothing had a small label attached to it, and it's marked with the room number. If you need laundry done, you would go into the bathroom, and there was an entry and exit tube. Dirty laundry would go to the laundry room via the entry tube, the clothes pulled out by a vacuum, and washed. They would be sent back through the exit hole, and appear in your clean clothes basket on the same day. Very clever. These pipes went everywhere around the building, from every room. If you forgot about the situation at the moment, the building was an engineering marvel. It would have been almost impossible to rig up the heating, water and air conditioning, but that was why the walls were thicker than two people standing together. There were other luxuries as well. Although he hadn't noticed at first, but you could change how the mattress felt by flipping it over with a button against the bed frame itself. It was actually a double-sided mattress. One side was memory foam, for easing stiffness, and the other was springs, to increase comfort. If they hadn't been blasted by a nuclear bomb, this building would have been decorated with nice plaster walls, paintings and more. But the rooms were the same, even if they were worthy of a five-star hotel. The same bleak, grey concrete everywhere. But the views from the windows were astonishing, even if they just showed how hopeless his predicament was. He could see all the way to what could have been an unbroken building, sitting in a silhouette. Adam also realised that he had no idea where they got food from. He thought it better not to ask; it tasted real enough and that was fine by him. He became more relaxed, and he realised that people hadn't been talking to *him*. But once they'd seen him as unthreatening,—people would be led to be suspicious in these times—, people opened up to Adam, talking with him about things he hadn't known at all, and showing him the hidden niches of the building, they now called home. They weren't friends; even though everyone had a level of hostility, but it felt nice nonetheless. His mind was taken away from his dead parents, and that helped a lot. There were people who told him about the history, some of the leaders and the new leader of their little group, who hadn't told anyone his name. It was odd, but it was all taken for granted.

*　*　*

Khan leant forward in his chair, and studied the map spread out on the table in front of him. He looked at the only two points of significance, and then made his decision.

"Send them. Ensure that they kill them all."

"Yes sir."

*　*　*

As Adam was entering his room, he heard a small scuttling, or maybe even a shuffle. *Probably something in the pipes,* he reasoned. But how could you hear through solid concrete? Adam could tell that something was wrong, but he had no idea what it could be. He stopped himself from undressing, and instead put on some grey trousers and a grey shirt; he would blend in more. As an afterthought, he reached into his wardrobe and pulled out one of the knives he'd taken in the wasteland. He had washed it and sterilised it with the radiation kit, so there was no chance of more poisoning. He had hidden it in a hastily made scabbard constructed from opposing layers of tape. He took it out, and gripped it firmly. It felt better to hold it.

He still didn't know what he was doing, or what was happening, but he reasoned that safe was better than sorry. Slowly, he crept back out of his room, and slunk across the narrow shadows on the edges of the corridors. Adam thought he could hear a faint dripping sound, and after each drip he could hear an almost inaudible sizzling. That set Adam's nerves on a tight edge. He realised that he'd taken a while to prepare, and it was now deep in the night. *All the better for me then. Wouldn't look too good if a concrete coloured boy leapt at a man while holding a knife he had liberated from a dead shopkeeper.*

He still had no idea where he was going, but the tour had certainly implanted itself into his mind. He went into an elevator, and pressed the button for the first floor. He went down quickly, and from inside, he could hear the sizzling sound more audibly. Strange. Then he heard the drip sound from right above him. Very strange. He looked up, and was just in time to avoid the small drip of water that fell through a small hole that hadn't been there before. Except, normal water didn't eat through carpet, metal and concrete. The singular drop went straight through, and that was when Adam realised that there was something terribly wrong. A small eye pressed itself to the hole burnt by itself, presumably, and then a fang was visible, dripping with venom. Adam knew what that meant. He leapt away, as the venom went flying just in front of his nose, and hit the door, where it gouged a deep gash in the concrete. It was a very powerful acid, and Adam was grateful when the doors opened. He sprinted out, then stopped dead in his tracks.

There were these creatures everywhere, clinging to the ceiling, and scuttling along the walls. Their bulbous, strangely deformed heads swiveled from left to right, but came to a stop when they looked at Adam.

"Hi." The creatures looked on it with what might have been contempt.

"I'm not here to hurt you. Can you go back to your sewers?"

They didn't understand, but the insult was evident in Adam's voice and they reared up, full 15 centimetres and all, and hissed. Adam took the opportunity and bolted, heading in the opposite direction to where he knew the armoury would eventually lie. But there were other things to get through. He cursed to himself as he stumbled over a protruding floor rivet, and was forced to roll to save himself. He lost time, and took all the skin off of his right knee and shoulder. For once he thanked himself for using the treadmill and swimming pool daily. They wouldn't catch him, but some would definitely double back and try to trap him. He looked grimly at the knife in his hand. He knew it wouldn't be enough. He had to get to the armoury, where he knew there would be more ammunition to get rid of them. He sprinted harder than ever before, but a wall loomed up in front of him. It had been placed as a prank on the tour, and Adam cursed the building; there was no going back. But there was a slight gap at the top, where they hadn't placed cement, and Adam could continue down the corridor. With the agility of a cat, or a cat with three legs, Adam jumped, grabbed the top, and pulled himself up while using his legs for extra power. He squeezed through the hole, scratching his back badly. But the wall had barely slowed him down, even though the creatures would be faster. As he kept on running, he gingerly put a hand under his shirt and felt his back. When he drew back, there was blood on his fingers. He knew the pain would come later; he was fuelled by adrenalin at the moment. He remembered looking at a floor plan of the building, and he knew that after the dummy wall, it wasn't far to the armoury. He pushed on, only to find himself face to face with a quick left turn. He skidded, his shoes complaining under the wear, and he used his hand to push off of the wall, giving himself more acceleration.

His breathing was ragged, and the pain in his back was becoming more evident as he lost more and more energy. The creatures, rats, mice, whatever they were, were quite far away, but still scuttling after him. Adam looked back, and, steeling himself, ran directly at the doors to the armoury, using his shoulder to ram it at the lock. His already injured shoulder complained bitterly, and he blacked out briefly, but he could feel the door give way under him. He tried again, and he burst into the armoury. It was an electro-magnetic lock, and it snapped back into place behind him, nullifying the need for an alarm. *They really need to work on their security,* Adam thought to himself. He hefted a gun, but he couldn't trust himself to use it. There were also gas masks on one of the walls, which would be necessary for going out. He ignored them for now, and instead he picked up a club, made from polished wood and reinforced with iron. He was expecting the weapon to be heavy, but it was light, and it was perfectly balanced, which meant that Adam wouldn't tire easily. He also grabbed a sharper knife, which was heavier than his own knife, but he knew that a knife from a military-grade armoury would work better than a knife stolen from a hardware store. He saw an odd notch in the club, and Adam realised that he could clip a knife to the top and bottom, and use it to stab and swing. He attached them, and looked back to the door to see the monstrous creatures swarm in. They had burnt their way through the door, leaving several holes through which they could run in. Adam looked around, and saw a fire alarm, and an emergency alarm, on the wall. He smiled inwardly. *There could very well be a fire, and the fire brigade of the apocalypse would be nice.* He pressed both, and an awful wailing was sent through the building. He knew that people would be gearing up, but they would arrive too late. Some of the rats flew at him, their fangs already dripping with venom. Adam swung with the club, and felt the jarring sensation as it hit their bodies, decimating their ribs. They were killed instantly. Adam stabbed and slashed with a knife, while also using his club to get rid of most of them. When he realised that he was getting overrun, he gave up trying to not use anything too dangerous and turned his back on them to grab a grenade. There was a ripping sensation in his leg, and he saw a deep gash on his inner thigh. Thankfully, it hadn't hit the artery. He pulled the pin, and rolled it gently to the crowd of squealing rats. They looked at the live grenade in confusion; one of them even braved a touch.   B u t once the fuse had gone, all of them were simply blown into oblivion, the shrapnel tearing into their charred bodies. The explosion was ear-shattering, and Adam realized that he should have gone further away. He opened his tightly shut eyes - *When did I close them?*—and shook his head in a vain attempt to stop the ringing. The smell of blood was thick in the air, and Adam retched, the bile splattering on the floor. He drew a hand across his mouth, then wiped them on his equally dirty trousers. There was one more creature left, which had probably survived the explosion and the sound of the ammunition in the room exploding. *Not a good idea to throw a grenade into a room full of live ammunition.* The creature had stayed back, probably scared of the fighting, and now it came in cautiously. Adam threw the club at it, and watched as it was crushed. He then looked up, and saw a few men running to the armoury. They looked in shock, and they also looked sick at the smell.

"Nice night for a walk," Adam said, before promptly collapsing.

He woke up in a hospital bed, with cloth in his ears and an IV needle in his left forearm. He was swathed in bandages and he could feel some sort of ointment under them. He felt groggy and dull, and his mind struggled to remember why he was here. A doctor in a white coat and glasses walked into the room. He tried to speak, but his tongue refused to move, and he could only watch, helplessly, as the doctor stuck another needle into his right arm, and he drifted away into unconsciousness again.

Adam looked up, and found himself in his own bed. He wondered how he'd gotten here.

The laundry chute? he wondered, his first attempt at a joke after waking up feeling horribly. His shoulder still ached from the roll, and his back was still hurting horribly. He must have not been given painkillers. Adam knew that something was going to change, no matter what. He would be recognised for his ability, and the only logical step for him was to become one of those black clad figures who go outside. At the start, Adam resented their presence, but now he was almost eager to become one of them. He'd seen the armoury, and he wanted to be one of them now, no matter if they'd shot him.

*   *   *

They came for him that night.

Four of them, walking slowly and purposefully, with a small device in the right-most person's hand. They walked up to the door, wreathed in the shadows of the darkened corridor, and pressed the odd-looking device into the card reader's slot. It would take thirty seconds to read the imprints left by the real card, and apply them to the fake one, allowing them access into the room. It was sophisticated technology, far ahead of its time. One of them shifted slightly, and said something inaudible.

Adam could hear them. See them. But he wasn't actually in his room. He was outside, just around the corner. His room was almost at the edge, so he had just wanted to make sure that there were no threats. Even though he knew he was acting crazy, he still wanted to make sure. And it had paid off. He knew that there would be someone who resented his presence there, someone on the inside who would want revenge. And he saw them standing outside of his room, burning a credit card in the slot to allow him access. Adam had only realised that this might happen mere minutes ago, and had only had time to lay a single device, that would hopefully trip them up, and end up with them cracking their heads on the concrete. It was a mop handle, secured tightly between the shifted bed frame and the bathroom door, and with the element of surprise, it might just work.

They opened the door, and immediately saw the target in the bed, under the covers with a mop of fair hair. What they didn't see was that it had been an actual mop. Adam had also found a small mop for cleaning in his bathroom cupboard, and it was very convincing. They were too occupied to notice the small figure slinking up behind them, and then shoving them all hard in the small of the backs. The men were on the verge of laughing, when their shins cracked into the mop handle. They didn't have enough force to smash the handle, but it had enough force to knock them down to the ground. Although the fall wasn't that bad, it stunned the men. They were surprised at this sudden attack, and that gave Adam all the opportunity he needed. He quickly slammed a small stone into their temples to incapitate them, but the third had recovered. He got up angrily, but a simple kick to the groin left him whimpering on the floor. The final man had stepped aside, and Adam ducked under the length of piping that had been swung at his jaw. He grabbed hold of it, and allowed the man to pull him closer, until Adam simply hit him across the jaw with a closed fist. It was far from boxing level, but he was still knocked unconscious by the blow. It was over. The other three struggled to get up, but simply nudging their wounds would send them into agony. Adam left them in his room, and went to go and find help, when the room number on the door caught his eye. It was glinting.

307.

He couldn't get out fast enough, and he didn't. A needle came out of nowhere and buried itself in his arm.

*   *   *

He groaned softly as he woke up. He was in a room, bound to a chair, with a gag forced into his mouth and his bound arms hand-cuffed together, and his legs cuffed to the chair. The room was small, with the chair he was in, a nondescript rug that looked worn, and concrete walls and floor. A bare lightbulb lit the room. Whoever these people were, they were taking no chances. Aside from the injuries he'd already sustained, his captors hadn't treated him with what you might call 'respect'. Someone heard him wake up, and as Adam looked at the man, he got up quickly and Adam struggled to track his movement from his chair. He was also foreign by the looks of it. As he got up from his chair, he looked at Adam with undisguised hatred in his eyes. He tore his gaze from the broken boy in front of him, and looked at the gun on the table in front of him. But, more worryingly so, he left the gun alone, and instead picked up a knife that was next to it. Adam's head swam as he thought about the horrible things that could be done with the six inches of sharpened steel that was being held by his kidnapper. Adam winced as he flipped it in the air, and caught it by the hilt cleanly. The man squatted down, and asked in a voice that would chill a wolf, "How did you do it?"

Adam could only shake his head, tears forming in his eyes. Who wanted to be tortured? His world had been rocked by the nuclrear explosion, and now this was happening. He almost couldn't believe his bad luck. The only logical fact he could find was that this was the terrorist's representative; after all, they were the only ones who were deemed responsible for this, right? But these thoughts were taken from his mind as he asked again.

"How did you do it?"

Adam moved his jaw up and down to mime talking, and the man ripped the tape from his face. Adam tried not to wince at the pain from this, and answered.

"What are you talking about?"

The man was none too happy about this. He leant down and asked again.

"How did you do it?"

"What are you talking about?"

The man then spoke again. Even if he was foreign, his English was impeccable. .

"Oh you just wait here; you will talk!" he spat at Adam. He moved away, and left the room in what was obviously anger. He returned with another man. But he was wheeling a trolley with him. It carried scalpels, syringes, knives and more. *I'm going to be tortured.* Adam was on the verge of hysteria, when the man wheeling the trolley reached behind him, and the gun in his holster was revealed. The handle and back of the barrel looked identical to the ones in the armoury back at the Arrowhead, and as he looked around in confusion, the camera in the corner had a red light beaming out from a small point. That settled it for Adam.

"I've passed the test now. What do you think?"

They looked at each other in surprise, then one of them started towards Adam. But the malice was gone. He simply wheeled the chair he was tied onto—*There were wheels the whole time.*—and walked out of the door, where there was a large corridor. Adam was wheeled out, and taken into his room after a few more turns. He was untied, and the door slammed shut behind the man. He sat back, and waited for something to happen.

*　*　*

A floor above where Adam lay, bound to a chair, three men were watching how things unfolded. Everyone could see the panic in the boy's eyes. They were about to call the end to the whole charade, when suddenly he looked calmer. He looked directly at the camera, and relaxed visibly. His next words shocked the three men into silence.

"I've passed the test now. What do you think?"

One of them spoke into a microphone that he just switched on.

"Take him away."

The two men in the room looked at each other, then one of them wheeled the bound boy out of the room.

CHAPTER 4

After a short wait, Adam noticed the door to the room opened, and a man walked in, nullifying Adam's guess as to a robot greeting him again. The man nodded at Adam, and closed the door behind him.

"You already know what that was for, and you already know what I'm here to say. You train tomorrow. Meet the rest of the training group at 0600 hours at the armoury. And by the way, the training group encompasses all of the Operators."

"Operators?"

"It's what we call 'those people'. In other words, the people who shot you when you broke into our building."

The man allowed himself a smile, and then got up to leave.

"And about that room; it's in the basement. It's used as a decoy for precisely this purpose, and all of the stuff in your wardrobe was fake."

He left, and Adam waited a few moments, and then left, where he turned towards the elevators.

*   *   *

The man known as Khan read the report that had been presented by the spineless man he called a butler. He'd hired him simply so that he wouldn't be scared of him, and yet even some of the strongest people would be scared of him. He laughed inwardly, but it had more aggression in it than a wolf laughing. He soon lost that inward smile when he read the words, "FAILURE" at the top of the report. He stopped reading, and asked his butler calmly, "How did they do it?"

The man shook when he addressed him, but he composed himself with as much strength he could muster, and replied.

"Our inside man said it was a child. That he got lucky. But the people in there don't think so, and they've made him an operator."

Both of them knew that this information was on the sheet of paper in Khan's hand. Both of them knew that the sheet of paper was a stage prop when someone like Khan was involved. Both of them knew who was going to be blamed.

"You organised this, am I right? I was sure that your military experience would benefit usgreatly, in these endeavours, am I right?"

The man could do nothing but nod meekly. With people like this, execution was all too common.

"But you have pleased me so far, and I do not wish to get rid of the only man who could serve me a drink and help me conquer the world that is alive within four hundred miles."

The man almost let out a sigh of relief, but he managed to rearrange his features to one of utmost terror like before, before Khan noticed.

"Now get out of my sight before I change my mind."

The man left, although his gait was almost unnoticeably faster.

*   *   *

Adam woke up early, at almost 5 AM, and took a quick shower, and he opened his wardrobe and wasn't even mildly surprised to see all but one set of the clothes he'd worn before, and they were replaced with the black uniform of the Operators. The garments were soft, and yet they were heavy, and Adam thought that there might be bulletproof padding, but it would have to be very thin. He pulled on the new black trainers to replace the blue ones, then ran downstairs to the cafeteria where he could see about forty of the Operators, queueing for food, or simply talking amongst each other. Adam grabbed some food, and sat down at one of the single-seated tables, and within ten minutes, his plate was empty. Adam placed it on the conveyor belt to the kitchen, and made his way to the armoury.

There were many people there, but only one or two acknowledged his presence and introduced themselves. A shorter man, actually shorter than Adam was, called David, and another man who was only a bit older than Adam, called Ben. He would be teaching Adam everything that he would need to know.

An alarm beeped once on everyone's watches, which had been coded differently for the Operators with different functions. Then, everyone began to walk down a corridor, through a series of twists and turns, until they reached a solid concrete wall. Someone touched their ID card to it, and the wall retracted, revealing a large gym. But this one contained fighting rings, and the weights were replaced with headgear and gloves, while a small shelf on the back wall contained gumshields. Adam could only stare, and now he realised why his map had a blank spot, which had been seemingly solid concrete. Everyone took up some padding, and paired up in the multiple rings. They started with free-sparring, where it was one on one the entire time, but Adam was being run through the techniques by Ben.

"Let's try the front jab. Side on, and aim down the arm at my hand. Step into it, and use your back, shoulder and legs to get all of the power possible."

It turned out that Adam learnt quickly, and that he could keep up with most others after a small amount of training. Everyone changed pairs, and soon Adam was paired up with a man of similar build to himself. Being the new recruit, the man had gone easy on him, until Adam floored him with a right hook to the jaw. If they hadn't been wearing padding, the man would have been out cold. The man smiled as he picked himself up, and they fought harder. Adam kicked out, and hit the man across the shins, and as he doubled over in pain, Adam slammed an elbow into his stomach. The fight was over, and Adam helped pick the man up, and they switched pairs.

Adam left the session bruised and battered, but pleased. He was learning quickly, and he knew that he would be able to get some form of vengeance on the man who turned his home into a wasteland. Adam could expect that people wouldn't know what had happened until a few days later, when they realised that the lack of communications would worry other countries aroud the globe. Someone would send a plane, or a drone, that would inevitably be destroyed, which would mean that the people in the Arrowhead would have to make contact, which was impossible due to the radioactive smog coating the city.

"Khan. That sounds like a video game character, not a terrorist. Let's see that photo, then."

Adam was again in a training session, after about a day or so, but this wasn't fighting. No. This was a sort of information lesson, in which he, along with a few other newer Operators were lectured on what their job truly was, and what they would be expected to do in their new position as an Operator.

"We have figured out that the leader of the terrorist organisation responsible for this is named Khan. He has no second name, but his details are all on the police databases that we have been able to acquire. He is a megalomaniac, and has been diagnosed with schizophrenia and other mental disabilities, and also has a higher-than-average IQ score."

They went on to talk about other things, but Adam knew that they wouldn't do him any good. The man droned on, and the lecture ended to give way to lunch. Adam ate quickly, and met Ben at the doors to the cafeteria.

"Follow me." Ben told Adam. Then, he walked off, winding down corridors, with Adam at his heels.

"Where are we going?" Adam enquired.

"Just wait. It's a secret." Ben replied craftily.

They walked on, and Ben opened a door. They went in, and Adam stared in shock. In front of him was the target range. There were different sections, one with moving targets, one with simple standstill targets which looked like the full head and torso of a person, with the bullseye just over the heart. The last section for close-range simulations.

"Wow." was all Adam could say.

Ben didn't say anything else as they walked onwards.

They went together to the armoury, which connected to the shooting range. It was much cleaner than Adam's last visit, the creature's blood gone and the concrete which had been shattered by the grenade was repaired. Along the walls were the melee weapons that he had used, but there were also some guns, which went across the wall on hooks.

"First up," said Ben. "the R4-C. 860 RPM fire rate, and can be used on semi-automatic mode by flicking this switch." He flicked a small switch on the side. He then handed the gun to Adam. "Don't worry, there's no ammunition in there. And flick the safety on the side. Stops the gun from firing."

Adam gratefully flicked the switch, and relaxed a bit.

"Next, we have the GSh-18 semi-automatic pistol. This is kept at all times with the operator in a holster, unlike the R4-C. There is, however, a sack to hold it in on your back as part of your gear."

He tossed the handgun to Adam, who caught it deftly. He also gave him a holster, which he equipped to his belt, and slid his gun in. It fit perfectly.

"And now, we have the other things. Grenades, smoke bombs, the usual. And a combat knife, which can be used in messy close combat."

Ben then grabbed some ammunition for the guns, and passed them to Adam.

"Alright. First on the agenda, you need to learn how to assemble and disassemble these guns, so you can unjam them, or just clean them. So, you take hold of the top…"

It took Adam about an hour to grasp how to disassemble the R4-C. Then, he had to put it back together, which was easier said than done. It was essentially a massive puzzle, and when Adam finally finished, he had to do it again. This time though, it took him barely ten minutes, and when he was finished with the R4-C, he had to move on to his GSh-18, which took barely any time, as it was a well-designed gun, and was very light and simple. Then, came the part which Adam had most been looking forward to. The actual shooting. When Ben had finally said that he was done assembling and disassembling the guns, he loaded the guns with the ammunition that Ben had given him, and took them to the shooting range, the GSh-18 in his holster, the R4-C in his sack.

"Then you need to know how to hold them properly. The GSh-18 is simple, right hand at the top, finger on trigger, gripping it fully, and left hand on the bottom for support. You want to place your feet shoulder-width apart, and your body is slanted to the side, like so." Ben demonstrated. "Then you can aim down the metal sights and fire the weapon. For the R4-C, you have your dominant hand on the trigger like the pistol, but you have a choice with your left hand." He produced a handle from his pocket. "You can grip the underbarrel like so," His hand was placed under the barrel of the gun, flat, gripping round. "or you can attach a foregrip." He snapped the handle to the bottom slightly in front of where his hand had been, and now he could just grip it from there. "You can aim down the sights, or attach a scope. You can also use a silencer with both the pistol and the rifle. You can just screw it onto the end. Finally, you can remove the rifle butt, which can make it more lightweight and compact, but sacrifices stability. You try it out."

Adam held the guns one by one, Ben making small adjustments to his grip and his stance when holding the guns, until he was satisfied with his posture.

"Now you need to know how to reload and use the *tap rack and roll* technique. The technique shows you how many bullets you have left, and if you have a bullet in the chamber.

For the GSh, you push the magazine release button, which can be done by using your thumb, and it drops out. Then, taking the magazine from the grips, you can just slam it in like so." He demonstrated. "It's much the same with the rifle, but you need to pull out the magazine yourself." Adam tried it, and after a few attempts was fluid with the technique. He then learnt how to check if there was a bullet in the magazine. "Now shooting. You don't want to push too hard on the trigger, you only want to tap it. Let the mind do the shooting. If you push on the trigger too hard it jerks the weapon, and you go off-target.

Adam tried to forget the trigger, and just aim down the sights, and after a few wayward shots when he'd moved his hand fractionally, he was hitting the target consistently. Adam then reloaded, and tried shooting all of his bullets at once, and they all tore into the target. Ben slowly increased the distance, until Adam was comfortable shooting his pistol when it was as far as a pistol would be accurate; pistols were highly inaccurate, unlike what the movies would say, Ben had told him. He then switched to his rifle, and he now knew what to do. He was able to hit the target quite often, and was soon perfectly accurate. He then

moved on to single-handed shooting, which required a looser grip, or else the gun would buck and break the wrist.

He soon mastered most of the techniques of shooting, but he was still slightly inaccurate, and he would have to iron it out with practice, but Ben was satisfied with his shooting. He then went on to show him some of the simulators, which were very realistic, and had Adam stand on a circular treadmill. This contraption was suspended in a large hamster ball, so that if Adam fell, it would be simulated in the VR goggles. He held a plastic knife, which was attached to all of the walls with cord, and it could simulate resistance against the knife too. All of the Operators used it to learn knife fighting, and at the end of their session there, Adam was already adept, learning how to disarm a knife wielder, and to use lunges and slashes to disarm a target.

By the end of the day, Adam was exhilarated, and he fell asleep instantly, savouring his progress. He wasn't fazed by killing; he'd asked Ben when he had doubts. He soon realised that the people he would be up against took everything away from him, and they were murderers.

"You wouldn't call a SWAT team murderers, would you? And yet they kill. It's just like that."

He had been given a bullet-proof vest, that would be worn in daily living. It was lightweight, and was made out of liquid body armour, which could stop a sniper bullet, if it wasn't armour piercing.

Breakfast was perfect, his eggs and bacon cooked to perfection. Other people talked with him, and congratulated him on becoming an Operator. Some people even looked up to him, or at least Adam thought they did. Some of them fist-bumped him, while others chatted with him, sharing jokes and banter amongst themselves. Training was also fun; they were in the gym, and a group ran on treadmills, while another group used the machines on a rota, while another group used the weights, and everyone rotated. By the end of it, Adam's muscles were on fire, but he noticed that he was able to do more than the others, some of them flagging on the treadmill, or hastily lowering weights after a few seconds. Adam had thought he would be hopelessly outmatched, but it seemed as though he was a welcome member of the group. To Adam, the day simply flew by, and the faces also flew by; literally. People were pulled out into assignments, some of them came back. Adam soon got to know everyone, and made a few friends. Ben, and another teenager called Kaspar. They rotated on assignments too, but Ben was usually around to teach him something new.

On the top floor of the building, an old man with greying hair and glasses sat at a polished wooden desk, typing at a state of the art computer, one of the many things that were unexplainable about the place. On his desk, absurdly, stood a name placard, which read "C. Charles". What he was typing about was a report, which had come in from one of his Operators, who was supposed to be looking over the new one. He double-clicked on a file, and began to read. A single eyebrow raised half way through. This might seem as mild surprise, but for people like C. Charles, it was the equivalent of a shout. He stopped, and began to type out a letter in response.

*　*　*

"Sir?"

Khan didn't even look up. He knew who it was already.

"We got word back from our inside man. Bu-"

Before the man could continue, Khan swore, and then began questioning.

"How did they survive those rats?"

Khan had seen them attack with a madness like no other. In a frenzy, they hacked, scratched and bit at all enemies, and there was a ruthlessness in their attack that was chilling.

"There was a boy… "

"How did a boy do anything against them?"

"Our man didn't see it happen. They say the boy is gifted. The bad news however," the man continued hastily, to avoid another interruption. "The other creatures in our labs have realised what happened. They won't enter the building anymore. They don't want to die."

"Kill them all, then."

The man left the room.

*   *   *

Adam's training had finally come to a point where he would be assigned randomly. It had said so in the letter that he found on his bed. He knew that he could be pulled out at any time, so he began to up his training.

In the next few days, Adam had just been focusing on exercise, upping his strength in the gym and firing one handed. He also practiced fighting more, and he soon grew to be one of the most prominent unarmed combatants in the entire building. And the time he spent paid off massively. He could feel more confident about an incoming assignment. And when it came, he was ready.

In another two days, he sat in the briefing room, with Ben, Kaspar and seven other people he didn't know. They all sat around a table, facing a plasma television screen on the wall. It flickered into life, and a voice rang out.

"This is a larger assignment than normal; we need to take ground away from Khan. As you can see, there is a section of land that is controlled by Khan's forces, and that place would be instrumental in leading an attack on the Arrowhead. You can see it on the map here."

The blank screen now showed a map, with the Arrowhead marked. It was clear that the small position that Khan had taken would definitely hurt a lot, if they didn't take it back before an attack could be launched.

"You will try to push back, unseen, and capture their supplies at the camp. There will be patrols, but we have a heat map in the mask screen. You can use it to locate the hostiles. Once you have captured the supplies, press the green button on the inside pocket of your jackets; it's a button to call for reinforcements. Press it once the supplies are taken, and we can overrun them and take the area for ourselves. Understood?"

They all nodded.

"Then go."

CHAPTER 5

The group went to the armoury and suited up, grabbing their rifles and their ammunition belts from the walls, and then slipping the gas masks onto their heads, where the sealing agent wrapped around the necks, stopping anything from entering from below. Adam looked at himself in one of the glass windows, the night sky able to reflect himself. He looked just like the others now.

"Mic test 1."

They had given each other numbers so that they could say less to convey more. Adam then held his hand to the side of his mask, and said,

"Mic test 2"

The others counted off, and once they were satisfied, they went out to the airlock. They opened the circular doors, and they all went in. They waited a couple of seconds for the doors to close behind them, then the front doors opened out to the outside world. Adam relished the feel of the fresh air, but the mask didn't help. He could tell that the others liked it outside too. The front doors closed behind them, and there was a hissing sound as all of the air was sucked out of the airlock and expelled into the outside, and a small click as a hole opened up in the corridor, to pressurise the chamber. They came in formation, and began to run quietly, blending in with the pitch-black buildings with ease. There was no moon, and that helped to look more hidden. There was a small map in one of the eyes of the mask, and they all spread out evenly until they reached their respective positions around the camp.

The place was dark, but there were some lights on around the place. They could see Khan's men milling around on guard duty. They looked raggedy and unkempt, and they all wore gas masks over their mouths, but not over their entire body; some of them wore short sleeves, exposing themselves to the radiation.

And bullets, Adam thought. They screwed on their silencers, and moved quietly. At the press of a button, a heat map was shown in their visors. It showed heated blobs spread around the area, which would be the Operators, and there were slightly colder blobs milling around the camp. There was an inaudible rustle behind him, and he saw one of the Operators climbing a tree for a better point of view. He also hefted a sniper rifle over his shoulder. A command came over the speakers in the mask, and they all moved forward as one, creeping slowly to not attract attention. There was a watchtower on the other side, and Adam realised that they were attacking with their backs to Khan, which was clever and stupid. Khan wouldn't expect them to attack from here, after all. Adam stopped thinking about it, and waited. There was a small flash of light from the muzzle of the sniper rifle, and the man in the watchtower slumped in his chair, as though he'd fallen asleep. When someone went to investigate later, it would be obvious from the large pool of blood on the ground.

The shot was their signal to move forward. They had the site surrounded, and they moved forward into the area. Adam was the first to encounter a sentry on patrol. He snuck quietly, while the sentry snapped branches underfoot, and as he turned the corner behind a building, Adam pounced, and wrapped his arm around the man's neck. The others arrived soon after, and the man was bound to a post securely, and gagged. He wouldn't get out ever, and they could come back with him as a hostage. They went further in, and soon they had taken about a quarter of the area. Most of the sentries had been taken, and the watchtower was down as well, which meant that they could attack properly. They went inside one of the broken buildings that had been rigged up for living space, and a few muffled grunts left the room. The men inside were tied up and gagged, and one of them had been shot just before he could sound the alarm. They continued on, and there were the same muffled sounds in the building next to them as the other five Operators did the same. Soon, there were about forty people left in the outer tents, and Adam told everyone that he was pressing the button. They waited until they could see the signal, which was four sparks from a lighter, and they attacked.

What they hadn't realised was that the signal had been faked. One of Khan's men had gone into the bushes and shown the signal, and although it didn't look like it, the rest of the men were armed to the teeth, and were ready to fight. The ten of them ran out, and were instantly confronted by a wall of gunfire. They all dove behind cover, the solid concrete blocking the bullets, but Adam knew that they would be outnumbered. He fired a shot over the concrete, and one of the men crumpled and lay still. He drew his pistol back as a spray of return fire came, and he heard someone cry out over the communications unit as a bullet grazed their helmet. Adam slapped the button again, praying that they would arrive in time. He shouted over the sounds at the group of four behind one of the concrete walls.

"We'll go back around the building and flank them!"

They nodded their understanding, and staying low, they went all the way around one of the ruined buildings, and began to shoot at the men. They shot methodically, and spent little time aiming, since they were all in one place. The men were just shooting with wild abandon, the recoil often jarring one of them to the ground. But they could still shoot straight. The men realised what was happening, and sent their efforts away from the group of six behind a container and at the small group attacking them. There was a burst of suppressed fire, and Adam estimated that they had taken out about ten of the men in the confusion. They began to shoot at whichever target they wanted, and soon both of the groups were forced to hide as two groups double their size advanced. Adam threw a smoke grenade down, and his group ran quickly over to another building, flitting like birds. The men were completely lost in the smoke, and once it cleared, one of them had been hit by another. They left him behind, and began shooting at where they had been. Adam and his group, which he now noticed included Kaspar, sprayed into the group, and the group of ten or so was defeated, their rusting guns falling out of their grip as they face-planted into the ground. They were finished off, and they moved on to help out the other group, which were being forced further and further back, and with a jolt of anger, Adam realised that one of the Operators was slumped, and was being dragged back. He was about to attack, when a sea of black figures poured out of the shadows, and Adam almost cried with relief as he saw them as the reinforcements. Together, they decimated the rest of the men, and also helped the man who was slumped. A bullet had taken him in the shoulder, and he was blacked out from pain. He was bandaged and placed on a stretcher, and the rest of the men saw the reinforcements and fled before they could be killed like the others. They realised that they were surrounded. And they gave up, throwing their guns into the bushes. They were bound as well, and soon they rounded up all of the prisoners, and the supplies like food and such, and went back to the Arrowhead. What the tour hadn't said about the cells in the basement, was that it was to hold people for interrogation. They began to march with their new captives towards the Arrowhead. This was another success against Khan, and they were all in high spirits. Unsuspecting, they continued.

But there were more men and before anyone could do anything, Adam was smothered with a bag, and a substance was sprayed on the helmet, short-circuiting it and causing it to black out, leaving Adam defenseless. and was yanked away from the group. Nobody noticed, and he was bundled into the back of a Jeep, and sped away into the night, following a rough track beaten into the dust. His only option left to him was in his pocket. He pressed the red button in his pocket. The emergency button.

The rest of the Operators heard the alarm go off as Adam pressed the button, and they saw the area where it came from on their heat maps. There was a very hot blob at the front of the group, and there were colder blobs behind it.

"A car!"

The full extent of what happened hit too late, and they knew that they would need another car or a group of cars to track them down, but the track would be mapped out and they could pick it up once they reached back to the Arrowhead.

*   *   *

The bag was lifted, but Adam kept his head slumped down, as though he was asleep, or unconscious.

"Get up. Get UP!"

A loud 'crack!' emanated through the room, and Adam woke up with a jolt, the side of his face stinging, as the sound of the slap faded away, leaving blood in his mouth. The sound still echoed against the metal walls. He sat up, the tape over his mouth preventing him from protesting or questioning his presence here. The man standing above him glowered down at him, and then Adam realized that he was lying down. The substance must have entered his mouth, and acted as a drug on him. The walls and floor of this room were similar somehow. He was dis-orientated, and he blacked out briefly. All of his energy was drained, and he could only lie there, and listen to whatever the hell Khan's men wanted from him. Then his vision sharpened, and he saw Khan himself, standing over him.

"No…" he said, his voice too weak to be heard through the tape, and he couldn't say anything more.

He ripped the tape off from his mouth, and he could see blood on the tape, which he threw behind him.

"Who are you really? How did you do it?"

Adam was weakened by the drug and the slap now, but he held his tongue. He was experienced now, and his fear was suppressed. He knew that he would be able to keep his mouth shut, and that was all that mattered.

"How did you do it!" Khan was shouting now, and he drew his gun. "I said, HOW DID YOU DO IT?"

He cocked his gun and aimed it right at Adam's head. He was too tired, too drained to do anything but lie there and await his end. There was malice in Khan's face, in his eyes. He realised he was a madman, capable of anything.

Khan raised the gun, his grip on it like one would strangle someone. He looked Adam in the eyes, his eyes filled with anger and malice, Adam's with defiance and hatred. His finger tightened on the trigger, and there was a loud bang, as the entire building began to shake. Khan stared around in what looked like profound confusion, and then understanding dawned on his face. He swore in what might have been Russian, and then he ran out of the room. Adam could hear shouts, and he heard the coughs and splutters of at least four cars' engines. He heard them drive off, and he was finally safe. But another splintering crack, as loud as a gunshot went off, and Adam managed to get up onto his elbows to see half of the ceiling in the room fall down. He feared that there was some earthquake or something, but three Operators came through the ceiling window, and rappelled down. They picked him up by the arms and legs. Adam was too tired to resist, and as his head lolled to the left, he could see the remnants of the ruined building collapsing.

The Operators were torn.

They only had just enough fuel to get back to the Arrowhead, and if they tried to pursue Khan, they would end up stranded in the wasteland. Their only choice was to head back, but letting Khan go seemed wrong, twisted. They really had no choice, but to leave it. They trudged back to the vans, down and dis-heartened, and drove back to The Arrowhead, tyres kicking up clouds and plumes of dust, and when it settled, they were gone.

* * *

Adam woke up back in the Arrowhead, the grey-green sunlight fading, waking him up; rousing him from his slumber. He was bruised all over, and there was still an imprint of a bruise on his cheek. He got up, groaning, and he realised that he had also twisted his ankle. He didn't feel as much pain as he did before the Operators rescued him, and that was probably because of the magic of the hospital wing in the building. He took a shower, and went down to eat breakfast with the others. He was applauded, and quite a few of the others were really shocked, as though what he'd done was amazing. Which in a sense, they were right. He had led the attack on them, and he had flanked them himself, but it felt weird to be the centre of attention. Adam was also still tired, so he took a day off from training and just slept, and his body thanked him dearly for it.

*   *   *

Khan was boiling, the ever-present madness in his eyes bubbling and the anger eminent on his face. He hadn't gained any intel from the boy, before he had been rescued, and that one child took out so many of his men. One of the only men who survived and managed to take him out, said that he had pressed some sort of button on his wrist, and then after about two minutes the cavalry arrived. He realised what it was. His man on the inside had never said anything about a panic button. He would have to be punished. But as for now, that boy. Adam, yes. He had to die, for humiliating him and his men. He already knew the location and layout of the Arrowhead, thanks to his man on the inside, but he was yet to gain important information about how exactly to overwhelm the Arrowhead and take control. He sat back, and vowed that he would get his revenge.

CHAPTER 6

They went through the forest silently, rubber soled boots feeling the ground for twigs and guiding the heel down to earth. They were crouched, and they had guns aloft, aiming everywhere and nowhere. One of them, in the lead of the group of five, went to his haunches, and studied the ground in front of him. A shift of the normal pattern of dust, and a slightly flattened part where the track had been covered up. This told him that he was still on track. Signalling to the others, he went onwards, and the group continued like this for about an hour. Then, a low rumbling noise came. After a short time, it was evidently an engine. Now they knew where to go. The lead tracker signalled again, and they went onwards, less careful about noise, since it was being masked by the engine. Soon, they reached a summit of a hill, and the group looked down on the scene below. About forty people were congregated, and they were clustered around a large, cube shape, that was being dragged by ropes across the area. It was a protective guard, and the weapons they used were completely random. Some held small pistols, others held rocket launchers, and they were an untidy rabble around the object, pushing and shoving. It would be a matter of time until someone accidentally fired. One of them then took off their gas mask, and then stripped down their all black uniform to reveal similar clothes that were being worn down at the summit. With a brief nod, the other four raised their weapons and the fifth went slowly, a smaller gas mask strapped to their face. He crept down, and used small dips in the hill to hide from people looking back. Soon, he was in the group, and he held a rusty gun, borne with scratches and a large dent in the stock. He surreptitiously came closer to the package, and simultaneously slid a hand into a pocket. There was a small, almost pin-sized camera, and a small dart shooter, which was completely silent. He shot the shooter, and a small wad of goo with a single circuit board, the size of an ant, encased in it, was shot through the crack in the cuboid packaging and sent into the box, hitting the cargo and sticking to it. It was new technology, and hadn't been used until now. He then stuck the camera in, and flicked a miniscule switch, all in one movement as though he was stumbling. Someone cursed at him, but the movement had been hidden.

The group finally reached the lorry, and half of them set about lifting it up into the back, while a few of them set about keeping watch. Then, once it was pushed all the way into the back and secured, all of the men went inside of it, shrugging off their heavy guns. What they didn't realise, is that they had momentarily had an extra man. And what they didn't realise as well, is that that moment had passed. The truck rumbled away, and revealed a single man, lying underneath where it had been. He got up, and ran back up the hill to where the rest of the Operators had been. The mission had been a complete success, and he was returning to the Arrowhead.

But then there was a soft *whumph* noise, and a dart-like projectile whistled out of the air and struck him in the back. He didn't have any time to scream, and slumped to his knees at the top of the hill. The last thing he saw in his life was four black-clad figures, blending into the night.

*   *   *

Adam had heard of the news about the scouting mission. It had been a man called James that had been killed. But apparently, the mission had been a success. Adam didn't even know what the mission was, but he hoped it would help their predicament right now.

After a day, he got his answer. He received a message that there was a meeting that was happening in the main briefing room at twelve. He finished his breakfast and he went down to the meeting room, where he found that all of the Operators were here. This was not a good sign.

"As you all know, we had a scouting mission a few days ago. We lost a good man that day, but he has played a vital part. He placed tracking devices on a large package, and inserted a microphone into the box. We have figured out that it is an EMP device."

There was a collective shudder throughout the room. They all knew what an EMP was. It would completely destroy the electronics in the building, and it would leave them dead on the ground, completely vulnerable to further attacks from Khan.

"As you know, this would be disastrous. We need to disarm it now. All of us will be there, and all of us will be needed to disarm it. We can reasonably estimate that there will be a massive armed force, to defend it and escort it into position near enough here to completely disable our electronics. Most of our sights on our guns will be gone. And the air conditioning will be stopped. Radiation will be let in. We need to stop them now.

We plan to flank their force, and have another force from behind, so that they are focused on us. Then a smaller group can take care of the bomb."

This was shown on a screen on the wall. Then, a large red pillar went up into the imaginary sky.

"That is what the EMP will look like on your maps. Follow it wherever it goes, and neutralize the threat."

Adam pulled on his black clothes, attached the body armour and his belt, slid his R4-C into his bag and various things like grenades, ammunition and his pistol into his belt and holster. He grabbed the gas mask, and ran out of the complex, around thirty others spreading out into the darkness of the approaching night. He ran softly, and glanced down at the GPS tracker which showed where the EMP was. He drew his R4-C, and dropped to one knee, while looking through the sight attached to the top. As he got closer to the site, he dropped to a crawl, while trying to keep an eye on his surroundings. There was the lightest sound of footfall, and Adam had never heard an Operator making a sound like that before, unless they were new recruits in training.

He whirled around, while activating his thermal sights in his screen. Carefully, keeping an eye on the direction that the twig had snapped, he drew his pistol, screwed on the silencer, and slipped his R4-C back into his holster. He took up a firing position, behind a tree, and leaned out to look in the direction. Looking around, he could see other heat sources, all moving in towards the EMP. These were probably the other Operators. Then, a blob of yellow and orange came out of a tree, and was in firing position. Adam fired, a wisp of a noise, and the figure snapped round and fell against the tree. Adam ran, and caught the body and lowered it to the ground before it could make too much noise. He reloaded his pistol, then glanced back down at his tracker. He then looked up with a jolt. They had been expected. He yelled into his helmet microphone, "AMBUSH! THEY'RE HERE!"

Some of them snapped around, looking for targets immediately, while others were slightly bemused, but the first gunshots rang aloud, forcing them into action. Adam moved onwards, and judging by his encounter, was guarded, and, leaving the thermal sights on, ran onwards to the site, making sure to avoid dry and cold ground. More shouts filled the air, and there was gunfire directed at him. Adam spotted a large rock nearby, and he rolled to it, narrowly dodging a bullet fired where his head had been. He drew his R4-C seamlessly and turned around to fire out of the side of the rock. He lined up his sight with one of the yellow blobs in his screen, and fired, then looked the other way and picked off 2 more of them. There were more people coming out of what looked like a van, or a bus. Adam primed an impact grenade that would explode on hitting anything, then threw it with pinpoint accuracy. He was aiming for the fuel area of the vehicle, as most vehicles had similar structure. A fireball spat out, and the shockwave of the fuel explosion threw many people aside. Adam took the opportunity to take his pistol out, aim down the sights and pick off the people on the floor, trying to get up. He ran forward to finish off what had been the backup troops, when he realised that the EMP was still making way onwards, and the force sent to deal with them had obviously been either held up or killed. That didn't matter, but what did matter was that the bomb was perilously close to the Arrowhead now, and would soon be in position. He shouted into his microphone again, and about ten others peeled away from the battle and headed away. The EMP was said to be behind them, and Adam turned around and went for it. There was a flashing red light in his screen, and Adam realised that he was looking directly at the grenade. It was a large slab of pipes and tubing, and there was a main missile-shaped section in the middle, which would carry the explosive. It was chilling to look at, but Adam focused his attention on the thirty or so people flanking it. Adam fired, and he saw two people slump. They had been standing right in front of each other. Adam didn't want to use grenades, which would have been perfect, in case they set off the grenade and took out their sights and electronic thermal vision in their gas masks, as well as the microphones. And so, he continued to fire, and with the help of the others, it was down to ten on nine. The men rushed the Operators, and Adam slammed the butt of his pistol into one's jaw, while he side-kicked another. Within seconds, the fight was over. The eight remaining ran towards the device, and one of them pulled out a tool kit and set to work defusing it. He left the others to watch over him, and went back to fend off more arrivals going for the bomb.

The men saw the EMP, and saw the shadowy figures surrounding it. They were overcome with rage and fury, and they lifted their weapons, trying to stop the people from destroying their plans. But they didn't see, in the dim night sky, the length of wire stretched across the area, secured to some boulders. They walked straight into it, and the wire-rope sprang free from its moorings, and wrapped itself around their group, until the two powerful magnets had linked together, and bound them tightly. Their weapons were held below by the wire crossing their arms, and they had to let go to dim the pain in their arms.

Then, another shadowy figure came out, and with fire glinting in the perspex eyes of the mask, he kicked the bundle of people over, and watched them roll away, until they fell into the ravine below. Adam looked back up, and could see other Operators running, some carrying MP7 submachine guns, and a couple holding out .45 ACP Vectors, the sound of rattling gunfire the only thing heard. He stood up, and drew his R4-C. He aimed down his sight, and picked off one who was in a melee battle with another. He then turned around to see someone sneaking up on him, and the man jumped in his direction, the flames glinting off of the knife in his hands. Adam ducked, the man flying over him, then elbowed him in the face, and he instinctively brought his hands up to his broken nose, his eyes filled with tears from the blow to the nose. Adam took the opportunity, and slammed the butt of the rifle into the attacker's stomach first, then the temple, and watched him sprawl to the ground. He turned around, while raising his pistol, and searched for another target. He took the ammunition from the belt lying on the ground that had belonged to the man he had just incapacitated , and swiftly reloaded his rifle, while maintaining an eye on his surroundings. There was a flash of a muzzle, and Adam instinctively dived into a roll as the bullet skimmed over his back. He sprang up and ran, making for the ridge in the terrain that sat not too far away, and was his only cover for a while. Although he might have a bulletproof vest, it wouldn't do much against a sniper rifle, and the impact of a bullet would definitely knock him out. He crouched as low as possible as a rock spat pebbles into the air next to him, and ran haphazardly to the EMP.. Jumping over a ditch and almost tripping over a body, he made it to the area, but he was a fraction too late, as he was knocked to the ground, the bullet knocking him back but his momentum taking him into the cover of the boulder. Expecting the worst, he lifted his shirt, but the bullet was embedded in his vest, but his ribs were severely bruised and maybe cracked from the impact. The vest was weakened, and it was pointless wearing it now that its structure had been broken. He slipped it off, and stretched his arms out as they thanked him for removing the heavy vest. He checked the magazine of his R4-C and reloaded it. Like an assassin, he rose from the shadows unseen, and took a shot over the boulder. He heard someone cry out, and knew that he had aimed in the right place. He switched the rifle to automatic, and emptied his magazine, turning the rifle marginally from left to right. He reloaded as he crawled over to the edge of the boulder to look out, then thought better as there could be someone waiting. He crouched behind the edge of the boulder, while using his spare scope in his pack as an attachment to his rifle's scope, which allowed him to look around the corner. He could see four shadows, holding guns aloft, waiting for movement. Adam drew his gun back, and screwed on a silencer, then he peered round through his scope again. Before they realised it, they were slumped on the ground, and Adam snuck out from the back of the boulder, and relieved the attackers from their ammunition, and he ran into the forest, and stopped. He'd sensed the man with some inhuman sixth sense, and halted to a sudden stop, as the knife flashed across where his neck would have been. Before he could react, his gun was wrenched from his grasp, and his legs were swept from under him. He jolted out of his stupor, and rolled to his feet fluidly, but as he was drawing his pistol, a hand chopped at his wrist and his fingers sprang open, and the gun fell from his grasp. He looked up to see a masked figure, with eyes full of hatred and intensity. Adam made a move at his side, but he was again knocked to the ground. He then feinted an attack to the man's left, and he grabbed at his hand, surely would have broken it, but Adam had his fist loosely curled, and he tightened it, and snatched it out of his grasp. The man was still watching his hand when Adam's foot twirled round and roundhouse kicked him in the jaw, and an elbow slammed into his ribs, and a knee to the groin. He staggered backwards under the onslaught, and Adam kept up the attack, swinging the edge of his hand into his neck. He was winded, and as he stumbled forward, Adam kneed him in the stomach. Gasping for breath, he fell to first his knees and then to his front. To make sure that he was down, he stomped on his knee, to stop him from going after him. Retrieving his weapons, he examined his ribs, which were definitely cracked. He was unconsciously wincing with every step. He opened his pack on his hip, and took out a syringe. This was filled with adrenaline, and he stabbed it into his thigh, and pressed down on the plunger. The pain became a mere shadow of itself, and he moved on, discarding the syringe. He was able to move faster, and he tapped the red button on the inside of his wrist, attempting to signal the alarm. But there was no sound, which meant that it hadn't done its job. The EMP was meddling with the electronic signal. It was a matter of time before it blew for real. He had to get out of range. He looked at the electronic map on his other wrist, and went in the opposite direction from the bomb. He repeatedly tapped the button on his wrist, but it wouldn't beep like it was supposed to. He looked up in vain, and then a hot streak of blood shot up next to him, and the pain hit him a second later. A bullet had grazed him. Wincing, he got up again, and ran back to the bomb, grabbing his gun again. He saw that the defuser was still working on it, and he needed more protection. There were others running to it as well, and there was a shout, as an explosion behind them propelled them into the air, sending them scattering like ragdolls. Adam landed with a thud next to the bomb, and he could feel it vibrating. He was powerless to do anything—he felt like a rib was broken. He struggled to his knees, and examined the bomb. It was almost crackling, and there was a whine emitting from it. It was increasing in pitch, and with it increased Adam's heart rate. The person working on it threw his tools down and shook his head. The message was clear. He drew his pistol, the pain in his chest even more evident. He had to be careful to not hit anything important, which could detonate the bomb early. There were two thick wires, and metal tubing everywhere. He used his thermal vision, and saw one of the metal tubes was much colder than the others. He took the chance, and fired. Gas escaped with enormous force, and the whole thing shuddered. Electricity crackled, and spat out of the pipes, and wires snapped under pressure. A bolt of electricity escaped out of it, and out of nowhere, a shockwave threw everyone around it a few metres away, into the wasteland. The sound of bones breaking, people screaming and cries for help. Adam twisted round on the ground, his broken rib screaming in pain. It was dark, but he realised it was because of the EMP—it had disabled the thermal visor. He swore to himself, then drew his gun and aimed at the shadowy figures advancing on them. He fired, and the figure came to a stop. Adam knew that he wouldn't be able to reload, and so he took each shot as carefully as possible, and he was supported by the rest of the Operators. They had defeated the rest of Khan's men, and had come back round to stop the EMP. The rest of them fell, and all of the Operators slumped in relief, and they all hobbled, stumbled or were carried back to the Dome, where the hospital staff awaited. Adam knew that he had stopped the bomb from exploding outwards, and instead triggered the explosion earlier, and also punched a hole in it to prevent it from exploding with too much force.

CHAPTER 7

Adam floated in a black, empty space, except it wasn't black; nothing was anything. It was hard to explain, but it was devoid of colour, feel and touch, his clothes unfelt on his body. He couldn't hear anything, and when he tried to speak, he couldn't hear what he was saying. After some time, a wind picked up, although he couldn't feel it, he could sense its movement. It blew into him and sent him spinning, and, mentally reeling, he closed his eyes, although the view wasn't much different. He felt himself slip away; but there wasn't anything different. He opened his eyes, but he sensed this was real; he was staring at a blank white ceiling with metal tubing traveling across the different beams of material. He didn't have the strength to keep his eyes open though, and the light was hurting them even more than the throbbing pain behind them. He closed his eyes, and soon fell into a sleep that was interrupted by dreams floating across his consciousness. After spending multiple weeks in what he later found out was the infirmary, recovering from his injuries, Adam was stiff, tired and generally just felt bad, but he put it aside as he got out of bed, and he walked the first steps in about four weeks. His cracked ribs had healed, and the doctors had said that his youth had saved him. His youth helped his ribs to heal much faster, and aside from a slight ache in his chest, he was fine again. He made his way back to his room, where he fell asleep in the softer and more comfortable bed that was there. He was exhausted by the effort and fell into a deep sleep.

He woke up more refreshed, but the pain still lingered in his body, like an unwelcome rash. It was similar to the last time, with cuts and bruises over his entire body. But the pain had already faded from his long stay in the hospital, and Adam felt much, much better. He was ready for action, his muscles no longer sore, and his head no longer hurting. He went into the shower, and felt the glorious sensation of the hot water streaming through his hair for the first time in a very long period. As he dressed, he realised that something was very wrong. There was a meeting in about an hour, but it said "ALL" on the screen of his mobile. That meant the civilians were included in that group. He had heard that none of them were ever included in the meetings; after all, battle tactics weren't the happiest of subjects in the world.

What is going on? he thought.

*   *   *

At the meeting room, there had been more chairs organised to fit all of the Arrowhead's inhabitants; voices filled the room. The people sat around, the Operators slightly confused and the civilians gazing around in awe, and some of them waiting patiently for someone to do something. The door to the room opened, and a man walked into the room. A small badge glinted on his blazer and Adam was sure that his name was written on it. He stood behind the lectern and waited for the voices to die down. When he began to speak, his voice filled the room even though he had no microphone.

"Ladies and gentlemen, we are in a time of peril; we are outnumbered, outclassed and outfought. We are close to being outnumbered and outgunned, and we have suffered large losses among our ranks. We won't stand for much longer if this continues, and we are the sole defence against Khan in his ulterior motive of taking over the United States of America. We need to stop him, and while we might have taken his forces out largely, it is no matter to simply get more. We can calculate that it would take Khan about a fortnight for reinforcements and to storm the Arrowhead. And we are left with only one option. To fight until our last breath."

Adam immediately saw a problem with this. *Why don't we call for backup?* Adam brooded over the thought, and the first problem was that Khan could trace and intercept the message, and potentially alter it. Another thing was that planes would be sent after the city, and all of them would crash and burn from the radiation. This would add to suspicion, and people might think that America had gone rogue. We could be a mistaken enemy, and targeted. After all, the government had fallen, there was nobody alive within America who could get word out; the attackers had planned for this, and they had planted it in the right position, so that when easterly winds came, the fallout would spread all the way across the country, without affecting others, so that they would be oblivious to the fact that the world biggest superpower had fallen.

Driving out?

Adam knew that they had working vehicles, and he guessed that it would be possible to take a group of communications staff and drive out in a fleet of cars that could support each other.

What about Khan?

Adam instantly had the answer to that question.

Operators.

He stood up just as the man, who was called C. Charles, according to the badge, was about to make his parting comment, something about bravery and serving the country.

"Sir! What if we call for backup?"

C. Charles looked at him as if he were crazy, or downright mad.

"Call for backup? How are we going to do that with the radioactive smog and the telephone lines cut?"

Adam had considered this too, but the solution was still the same.

"Drive out?"

To the civilians, it seemed as though Adam was joking. But the Operators began to nod assent. Adam was encouraged, and began to talk faster.

"So we take a groupof communications people that can make contact with a nearby country or even a Navy SEAL team or something, and they can be backup. We could get another four hundred men or something, couldn't we?"

"But what about Khan?"

"Take some Operators with the group to fend off attackers."

The man contemplated the idea, and Adam could see the spark in his eyes that showed that he was on board with the idea.

"Very well then; change of our plans. We will not waste our time with bravado, instead, we will call for backup."

The room erupted into voices, and C. Charles simply raised a hand for silence, and the noise cut off.

"We had told you that this wasn't possible, because of the radioactive fallout, but it seems that simply driving a car is the solution. We will take a fleet of vehicles, one of them holding the communications equipment to broadcast a help message, and another for Operators. The rest will be fuel-bearers, and will return once they reach half of a tank, after distributing the fuel among the group. More cars can make their way like this, and they will be fueled until the end."

Someone came up to the stage, and whispered something into the man's ear.

"There is an SAS unit in Alberta, Canada, and we can reach them in 40 hours."

The man made his calculations after he said that, while the crowd assembled cheered.

"Yes, it will take that long to reach, and it will take that time to come back, and also we need to account for border restrictions too, which could add on another day. So we could say, about a week, taking into account the encounters with the British government and such. We need to last a week. One more week, and we can finally free ourselves from besiegement. In that week, there will be basic training provided to all, to ensure that if it comes to the situation, all of us can fend for ourselves."

The man left the room as suddenly as he had come in, and questions filled the air, people shouting about unfairness, even asking what guns they got and others were simply moaning about everything and all. He couldn't stand listening to the din in the room; he already had a headache. But he stayed put, and tried to be helpful by answering questions and telling people what to expect. Soon, his head was throbbing painfully and his eyes were on fire. He left the meeting room and went to his own room. The noise was non-existent there, and after taking some medicine and resting, his headache was non-existent too. He then went to the armoury, where there were about sixty to seventy people crowding the room, some of them handling the weapons, some standing around with a bemused expression, and some were already trying their skills on the targets. There was a lot of noise as Operators tried their best to make themselves heard to their recruits, and there was a lot of signing going on. Some people looked bemused, some looked fascinated and eager, and some looked as if the entire thing was crazy and downright idiotic, looking with contempt at the Operators, or the weapons stacked on the walls. These people were left adrift; everyone could see that they had no interest in what was happening around them, and they were all given a wide berth. Adam spotted someone who looked slightly lost, holding the pistol he'd been given completely wrong. Adam stepped over to help out.

Everyone was grateful when the end of the day finally turned up. It had been exhausting, even for the Operators that hadn't been doing anything on the day; the noise and the new challenges proposed were simply mind-boggling, and it clearly pained other people to just think about it. The people of the Arrowhead fell into their beds gratefully, and not even the sadness that engulfed many of the people in the Arrowhead could break through their sleep. As the day finally drew to a close, all that could be seen was the glint of the light on the bulletproof plate glass that constructed the building.

In the morning, the same chaos reigned supreme, but there was some improvement. People found less reason to complain and get angry with each other, and they were patient and willing to learn. Progress leaped forward, and for once Adam felt in control of his own life, and felt able to deliver justice to Khan. But only on the second day into the time slot, the worst happened. A radio message had come over from Communications, and it said that the lead vehicle with the main brunt of the fuel was broken down, and there was no way to transfer it all to one of the other vehicles without wasting fuel that would be necessary to make the journey. It was the worst thing that could have happened that they had no control over, and it seemed like the only option would be to send a repair van out. But they needed protection too, and everybody was held up by the training. It seemed like a petty excuse, but some people were scared of the big action, and others were preoccupied with issuing weapons and teaching basic fighting skills. There wasn't anyone to help, and Adam knew that if there wasn't protection then they would be blitzed by either roadside mines or Khan's men. Adam decided to go with the repair vehicle, and when people were picked, he and one other Operator, who happened to be Kaspar, volunteered to go with the van and provide protection. He sent a message to the repair van telling them to wait, and he got his gear from the armoury and, with Kaspar, ran out to the van.

"Good luck to us, then."

The joke was to cover up the fact that both of them were very nervous. They leapt into the back of the front SUV leading the two-car convoy to the others, and they rumbled off into the dust, leaving more behind.

There were bumps, there were potholes and the ride was extremely tough, the suspension stiff to help with the road and speed issues. Adam was mildly regretting his choice in coming, but he knew that he could help, and he knew that his presence generated calm among the little group. Surprisingly, Kaspar looked a little queasy, but with what seemed like an intense amount of concentration, pushed away the motion-sickness. The SUV stayed a little ahead of the van, to either pick up the roadside mines for itself or to keep a look out for someone who might run the car down, or sacrifice themselves to get the van, and there was one person situated in the back behind four layers of bulletproof glass, looking out for people attacking from behind. They moved on, driving through the deserted roads and the ruined cities. It was an almost impossible gamble. If they were encased in one of the dust storms, they would be forced to stop, and that could cost their lives in the long run. And if they did make it to the area specified on the map, they could still be massacred by Khan's men. Adam cleared his mind and tried to get some sleep amongst the bumps and rattles as the driver put his foot down, and the vehicle leapt forward, propelled by the V8 engine in the front, powering the four wheel drive system.

The journey went smoothly; the only trouble they had was a few grains of sand inside the car itself, but they finally had the group in sight. It had taken many days of switching drivers and tentative naps, but they would be able to repair the vehicle and make it back to the base. As they drew closer, Adam's sixth sense was tingling. He forced himself to calm down, but in the back of his mind, he knew that something was wrong. There was no movement around, nobody inside or outside, and it looked desolate; the cars hadn't even activated their windscreen wipers to move the dust. He stopped everyone from leaving, and advanced himself with Kaspar. It was clear, even beneath the gas mask, that he knew that something was afoot. Drawing his gun, he knelt and aimed at the largest van there. Almost out of instinct, he looked at the license plate. All of the vehicles were coded with a custom license plate; F-J, then two prime numbers, then it would say L-P. They had picked up on this, but they had been too late to see the numbers, so they had chosen a random 4 digit number, and placed them on. He yelled out "IT'S A TRAP! GET DO-" before it happened. The furthest, and largest van had encased a massive bomb, and the outsides of the van were melting away to reveal the bomb. Adam dived behind their own SUV, and Kaspar sprinted to a nearby boulder. He plugged his ears, and prayed. The other vehicles were blasted away, but Adam was lucky in the sense that the car he was behind stayed put, probably because of the weaponry and spare tyre in the back of the van. But it rocked worryingly, and he heard the suspension coils snap, and the engine explode under pressure. Hot fuel and oil rained down, and Adam was forced to run. They still had the one van, the one that would be carrying out the repair, but there was only room in there for the driver, who would act as an assistant to the mechanic, and two more people. The rest of the crew were either dead or mortally wounded, but the van was fine. Kaspar emerged from behind the boulder, and Adam yelled into the microphone, "GET IN!"

He complied, rolling over a wheel arch that had just fallen in front of him and dodged a flaming rubber seal, and dived into the back amongst the repair equipment and tools.

"GO GO GO," he bawled at the driver, and there was a massive dust plume behind them as the driver gunned the engine, speeding away from the ambush site. Most of the others had died, only a few were alive, but only just. Adam knew he couldn't save them, and that there would be a second bomb to finish them off. Adam was able to take one more look out of the back, before the second bomb exploded, and the area around was flattened by the shockwave. He looked in mute horror, before lying down in one of the two hammocks strung in the tightly packed interior, and closing his eyes. It was a long way to the *actual* breakdown site after all. *The actual? What if it was just a ploy, to get us out? What if they never broke down?"* Then there was an infinitely more chilling thought. *What if they were killed?* Adam felt that the only logical conclusion was that it was a trap, to try and disable them, and the fact that Khan now knew that they survived would mean that the actual group would be killed in similar fashion. He voiced his concerns to Kaspar, who nodded.

"That's likely. They have no use for them, but how could they have known why there was a whole fleet of vehicles? How could they have known that the lead vehicle held all of the fuel?"

Adam's breath caught in his throat at the suggestion in his mind.

"Someone's betrayed us. They must have an inside man, within the Arrowhead, who gives Khan all of the information he could possibly want. And how would they know when to start shooting at us with the EMP? We were unseen, and suddenly I got shot at. Someone is telling them everything."

They had both paled; they knew that if there was an inside man, they would be dead, as dead as the rest of the people in the Arrowhead by the time they reached back there. In a coffin. Those were the thoughts that plagued all of the people in the cramped van. Then, after going as fast as the engine would allow for almost a hundred miles, they finally caught sight of the group. Adam shook Kaspar awake, and they leant out of the side doors to look at the scene that was presented before them.

The fleet was legitimate, and Adam recognized the number plates. Clearly, the impostor had neglected to tell Khan that the license plates were coded, and had just given him an example to follow. Adam almost smiled. The person who wanted them all dead saved their lives.

The fleet stopped as they saw the van racing towards them. Some of the Operators had taken defensive positions, but they stopped when they saw Adam leaning out. As they skidded to a halt, Adam leapt out, and with Kaspar adding facts in, explained the whole situation.

"We received a radio message apparently from you, telling us that you had broken down. Of course, it was from Khan, and everything exploded nicely once we reached the fake fleet. We got away and came to tell you the news. The conclusion that we came to was that there was a betrayer; an inside man for Khan."

"So that's how they knew?"

The man swore.

"So we will accompany you; the van has enough fuel to return, and I doubt that Khan will waste his efforts in taking it out. You can message the Arrowhead and tell them everything, and we will stay with you in one of the vans or SUVs."

"Any hitchhiker's will be ignored!" he laughed. But the laugh was forced.

CHAPTER 8

They went onwards, and judging by the maps, they were on the borders of Canada on the third and final day of travelling to the SAS unit. After about a hundred miles of actual, smooth roads to the border, they were stopped by a border official.

"My goodness your cars are dusty. And old. Where have you come from?"

"Not enough time to explain, sir." was the reply by one of the Operators. "Secret service."

They obviously weren't part of the Secret Service, but someone had conjured up a badge and decided to take it with them on the journey. It was clearly genuine, and the border official stepped back a little after he'd seen the rifle on the Operator's back, and ushered them through. They drove on, getting some weird looks from the locals, but they made their way to the destination down of Alberta. Most of them slept on the journey, and drove to where the database had said that there was an SAS team. When they entered Alberta, they drove around until they found it. It wasn't advertised, but it was clearly there, and there were a massive set of closed iron gates. Although the rusty gates were ominous, they weren't much of a protection. And although it didn't seem like it, there were much, much more things around. Pressure detectors, cameras, a garrote that could be lowered or raised to get motorcyclists, and a car lift that could be raised while a vehicle was driving over to hang it in the air, keeping it elevated. Then a man came out, and said,

"Welcome to Paul's Motoring Shop. How may I help you lot today?"

It seemed like they had found the right place, but there was one more last ditch effort. A code phrase. They had been given a phrase to tell anyone that would grant them access. Some people thought that it was because the man, "C. Charles, according to the badge" Adam had said, was British. They had been briefed on it by the other Operators, and Adam decided to take charge.

"A great day for a steak and kidney pie."

It was bizarre, but it was to avoid a phrase that would be used on a day-to-day basis. The man looked as impassive as ever, but then left abruptly, and an entire squadron of what were obviously military men came out, with guns raised. Adam and the other Operators holstered their weapons, and put their hands up. They were in a remote location, and if there was bloodshed here, nobody would know.

"Who are you?"

The accent was strange, and it sounded like the man was saying 'yeah' instead of 'you'.

Adam responded, "There's a bit of a situation back in America."

"We could tell; not many secret service men come in dusty Toyotas, eh?"

Adam cut to the chase.

"A nuclear bomb."

The men, who had been sniggering at the joke froze, and one of them spoke up."

"A kid with big dreams, right?"

But the rest of the Operators said the same things as Adam, and soon the leader of the group said,

"We'd best come inside for this. It's all a bit strange."

* * *

"So, your base is under attack by a terrorist organisation, correct?"

"Yes, and you were the closest reinforcements we could find. A hundred men would be enough, but any number above would help massively. We have sixty Operators available for action right now, and they are also training about forty more civilians. In total, about a hundred."

"I would be happy to provide one-hundred and fifty men for your services. And it's alright if they all don't come back in one piece. They're trained for this."

Adam sighed inwardly. It had worked.

"We need refuelling-"

"Ignore those rustboxes. We've got cars. We've got lorries. And, we've got gas masks."

It was about night now, and after telling the lead man, whose name was Larson, about the possibility of ambush, they all slept in still-moving beds for the first time in three sleepless nights. The beds did wonders for their bodies. They moulded themselves into the Operator's bodies, somehow supporting the bruises and stiff parts, while allowing the parts of the body that were fine to relax and seep into the mattress. It felt glorious, and Adam felt brand new after a cold shower and a change of clothes into the spare sets they all had. The men were suiting up, and after a British breakfast of eggs, sausages, beans and a completely new thing they called 'hash browns', they set off in much nicer cars, after changing the number plates to the ones written on the old ones. This was just to show the people of the Arrowhead that they were trustworthy. And these vehicles were much, much faster. They were averaging about ninety miles an hour, and one of the SAS people explained to him in their SUV that speed limits wouldn't matter; they would see the small badges on the fronts of the cars and know that they were SAS. As they made it past the hundred miles of non-wasteland, the SAS men were literally shut up by the levity of what had happened. The buildings gradually got more and more ruined, more and more dust began to coat the cars, and soon they reached a point where it was clear. They finally had to stop, since it was nightfall, and after a cold meal, they slept, some in the cars, some in small tents that they had pitched. When they left, they were in high spirits that they would reach on time. They would be about on time, which was perfect. They hit the vaporisation zone, when they all had masks on, and they could see the emptiness that was the Dome. Adam navigated the lead vehicle through the narrow pass that was invisible to an eye that hadn't gone through it before, and stopped in front of the main gates that were invisible. With a hiss, they opened up to reveal the complex of the Arrowhead.

"It's about time you came. We've got a war coming."

*   *   *

Khan paced the room of his main headquarters, as the man stood stock still in front of him, with the uniform of an Operator, and an air of superiority of him, although that was crushed whenever Khan was around.

"So, they've arrived, have they?"

"Yes. It was out of my power to stop them from entering the building."

"And the boy is alive, even from the ambush?"

The man was dreading the next bit of the conversation.

"He was… resourceful. He knew that there was an ambush before it happened, and was able to dive to safety."

"How did he know?"

"He told me. The number plates."

The man's voice cracked on the last syllable.

"What about the plates?"

"They were coded…"

That was all that Khan had to hear.

"You have failed me. But, you can still redeem yourself."

The man almost slumped to his knees in relief.

"You will lead the group into the battle, and once they have taken the brunt of my forces, and I have taken the brunt of their forces, we will be face to face. You then show your true colours."

"Yes, sir."

* * *

After a day of rest, they set off at midnight the next day.

Two hundred and forty seven people, running, both with their choice of weaponry. The Brits held Glock 17 pistols, and Heckler and Koch MP5 submachine guns. They had their own tactical gear in their vehicles, and they were as armed as the Operators. They spread out, heading for the location that they had found was Khan's headquarters.

There would be fighting, and there would be death, but it was all necessary. Ben was at the top, and they all went quietly, not making a sound other than the quiet sound of the boots hitting the ground at a jog. Then, all hell broke loose. The new trainees had been taught to not freeze up and end up dead immediately, and had been given a false alarm to show them the meaning of the lesson, and they sprang, still ungracefully, into action. There were gunshots, and a couple of their force went down, but the threat was neutralized immediately. It was more of Khan's men, and there had been a group of about twenty. A scouting party, clearly. Now they no longer had the element of surprise. They went faster, not caring for the sound. They had to make it there or be killed in the effort. Then a building loomed up. It was large, and squat, and there were several smaller buildings dotted around it. Clearly, the larger one would be for Khan, but even if Khan was trying to outplay them, they still had no choice but to stick together. But then the enemy emerged from everywhere; from the dead bushes, from the buildings, from the skies even. They were completely surrounded. Then the shooting began.

They all dropped to their knees, and this stunned Khan's men, for the opening salvo of bullets went right above their previous positions, and slammed into the other sides. At least twenty men were shot down by this, and another ten were injured. They redirected their fire, but by then, the Operator and SAS task force struck.

Bullets tore into the crowd, and seeing the issue, Khan's men ran at them. Swiftly, the front lines rose, while leaving shooting space for the people behind, and engaged in combat. Knives turned up, and Adam was grateful for the training. The new people were in the middle, while the real Operators stayed at the front lines. Adam came forward to the line, and began to fight. He ducked under a slash by a knife, and elbowed the holder in the neck while grasping the wrist and twisting it violently to the left. He was floored and stampeded. He kicked out, and also shouldered someone else. The disruptions caused more tripping, and quite a few of the forces fell flat on their faces, where they were taken by the ten snipers around the outside. Both of their numbers were dwindling, but Khan's men were going. But there were a large number of casualties, and when the large force was finally gone, most of the people were forced to stop and help the injured. The free remaining people counted up to about fifty. But some of them needed extra support, and some of them were almost dead at the back end, so another twenty had to leave. Thirty left to eliminate Khan. Grimly, Adam and the group set off, with Ben in the lead. They came up to the building, but Ben told them to ignore the front entrance, as it would be trapped, and instead led them round to the back. He then tore off his gas mask to reveal a smaller mask, and spoke.

"I'm sorry…"

Then Khan himself rounded the corner, and before anyone could react, they were seized from behind, and bound with cuffs and chains. The people who struggled were knocked out with heavy blows from batons, and those who didn't were shoved roughly to the floor. Adam looked up through the screen of his mask, into Khan's unsmiling face.

CHAPTER 9

"Get up. Now."

Adam hadn't realised that he'd fallen to his knees, but the fact that Khan wasn't shouting was even scarier than the gun pointed at his head.

"Take the mask off."

Adam tore it off, and threw it away, spinning it over before it clattered to the ground loudly.

"You might be wondering why I'm gloating now. Maybe because I beat you. Maybe because the United States is now my personal playground. Or perhaps, I stopped you people from 'saving the world.' Before you die, which I want to watch personally, there is just one more thing left to do."

He clapped his hands together once, and one of the Operators was pushed from the line. He looked very, very nervous. As though he had something to hide.

"This little person told me everything I needed to know to get rid of you. Everything that I needed to know about your little plans, scurrying around the place. He has done me well, and I just want you to know who did me such a service."

With shaking hands, the man removed his mask. Adam was shocked into silence.

It was Ben.

"I'm sorry Adam," he gasped.

"You've caused the deaths of millions of people. This was all a game."

"No no! I made a deal with Khan. He would spare me when he eventually killed everyone, and I would help him with that. I was never a terrorist."

"You're worse than one."

But then Ben's face hardened.

"You were always one to take credit for everything. Saving us all, getting the 'cavalry', this, that, outclassing ME. Who should put up with a boy, still in short trousers, doing everything that real men did?"

Now Ben raised his gun.

"I was too close to you in the Arrowhead. I wasn't able to get rid of you. And Khan didn't kill you either. What a mistake. So I'm taking it into my own hands."

He drew his pistol and placed it directly against Adam's forehead. His eyes were filled with malice, while Adam just looked at Ben with contempt.

"Goodbye, wonderboy. See you in Hell."

There was a bang. But Adam felt no pain. Maybe that was because Ben fell to the ground, a bullet implanted in his head.

"I want the pleasure, Ben. Not you."

Khan now aimed the gun at Ben.

"What are you going to do now? Dodge the bullet?"

He laughed, and his soldiers also laughed, after waiting to see if he would allow it."

Adam drew the canister of knockout gas. He aimed it directly at Khan.

"I've taken adrenaline shots. That won't work on me, silly child."

Then Adam took out the lighter he'd taken from Khan's pocket when he had pulled Adam up. Before Khan could react, Adam lit the lighter and sprayed.

A jet of flame encased Khan. He screamed, and his clothes were on fire. He rolled manically, trying to get rid of it, but the fire had already held. When he finally shook it off, his hair was gone, and his mouth was permanently curled in a snarl.

"You little rat! Do you think a fire can kill-"

Adam simply shot him in the leg, and while he was down, he ducked to avoid the inevitable attack from Khan's men. As Khan gasped in agony, the group struck out at their captors, and they were all either dead or out cold within seconds. They looked back at Khan, who had pulled his gun out of his holster with a bloodied hand. Adam kicked his leg, and he screamed. Khan's hand trembled with the effort of bringing the gun up. Adam's eyes instinctively widened.

Khan fired.

He had shot himself in the head, to stop the pain and to end it all. They went back outside to the injured, and an almighty cheer swept the crowd at their return. A squad came out from behind them and told Adam that they were coming for them when they heard the first gunshot.

"Where's Ben?"

"He's dead, Kaspar."

"What?"

"He was the traitor. He did it out of personal spite against me."

Kaspar was shocked into silence, and they counted the casualties and deaths among their group.

"Two dead, stampeded, one hundred and forty minor casualties, and eighty major casualties." they reported.

"All in all, an outstanding success. We can leave now. Go live somewhere else. This isn't our problem anymore, but who wants to stay and help?"

What happened next almost floored Adam with shock. Almost everybody in the crowd who had been living in the Arrowhead had their hand up. Adam had his own hand up, but now he realised that so many people had no family, or life outside of America. Now that the world knew what happened, there would be a rebuilding of America. New government, new rules, and new wars. And Adam didn't have to take any part in that. His job was to just relax. Maybe get an online job when he was slightly older. A memory bubbled up from nowhere. He remembered white clothing, shouting, and a belt. Judo lessons. It seemed so out of place now, but it fit in. Martial arts, and a dedication. He felt a pang of pain at the rememberance of normal times, But he had no need to worry about attacks, terrorists, or anything. He was finally free, and there was an immense lifting sensation in his chest. Almost as if he was being reborn. As they set off back to the Arrowhead, instead of feeling morose, they felt happy, and there were celebrations for dinner. Everyone, including the British, feasted. Wine bottles were produced out of nowhere. And the spare rooms were opened for the British to rest. After all, such a feast deserved a good room. There was a final cheer across the Arrowhead, before the lights finally went out, and the people of the Arrowhead slept easy for the first time in almost a year.

EPILOGUE

Rumour had spread that the man taking over America was killed by a child. The man who had just read the proof of this put the folder down, and rubbed his hands on his trousers. The man was the head of a secret organisation, who had funded Khan's rise to power. And he had failed them. It was good that he was already dead. It meant that the man didn't have to do it himself. The organisation had been one of the most sinister criminal scenes in the world, but they had used their bankroll on this one project, and now they were bankrupted. They were stuck. And it was almost hilarious how close one child got to death, and avoided it because of money issues. The man sighed, and opened the balcony door and stepped onto the balcony on the seventieth floor of the building. The building was empty. No point leaving evidence behind. The people had left to their normal lives. But the man had to go. He stepped over the railing and fell.